Hot SEAL,
Dirty Martini

SEALs in Paradise

CAT JOHNSON

New York Times & USA Today Bestselling Author

CHAPTER ONE

"As you can see, the view is amazing."

Like a shadow, or the stink that clung to the inside of a gym bag, the real estate agent followed Clay to the expansive picture window that faced the Pacific Ocean.

Clay made a non-committal grunt to acknowledge he'd heard the man, but didn't comment. He didn't mean to be rude to Russell Ramirez, real estate agent extraordinaire, but this was business. Hundreds of thousands of Clay's dollars were on the line here.

On the outside Clay remained cool as a cucumber. On the inside he was doing backflips, because even with as annoying as Ramirez was by being up Clay's ass throughout the duration of the showing, the man was right. This was one of the most amazing views Clay had ever seen—and that was saying something because he'd seen a lot in his twenty-years in the Navy.

The good news was the view came with a ramshackle bungalow that had seen better days. That was good news because it had a bargain price tag to match its downtrodden state.

The only reason a developer hadn't already snapped it up had to be the size of the lot and the zoning laws. The structure couldn't be added on to. Not up, since a second story wasn't allowed. Definitely not out, since the building just about rode the property line as it was.

Restoration of the original home was the only option, and that was fine because Clay had no intention of expanding. The house had character just as it was—unlike some of the other buildings he'd seen.

The 1950s single story, one thousand square foot bungalow located in Imperial Beach suited him just fine.

He didn't need or want more space than that. He'd lived in the bachelor barracks for enough years, he didn't have much stuff or need much room. Just a bedroom large enough to fit a bed and space outdoors for a barbecue grill.

What would he do with a big piece of property anyway? He sure as hell didn't want to spend his retirement years tending a yard.

Here, the Pacific could be his backyard. It was perfect. His own little piece of paradise.

"So what do you think?" the agent asked. When Clay didn't reply immediately, he said, "Mr. Hagan?"

It had to be driving the man crazy that Clay had yet to comment.

After two decades in the Navy, the majority of that time spent as a SEAL, Clay knew well how to bide his time. The team would prepare, and then wait. And then wait some more. Finally, only when the time was right, they'd jump into action and spring on their prey—which was usually someone who wanted them dead.

Compared to Clay's experience with armed insurgents out to annihilate him and all he held dear, one California real estate agent was nothing.

Clay lifted a shoulder and said, "I don't know. It needs a lot of work."

That was the truth, but it was mostly cosmetic. He knew the bones were good. The house was solid. Amazing, considering its beachfront location. It was a testament to the craftsmen who'd built it so many years ago. Back when quality mattered.

"It's the perfect restoration project for the right person." The agent was a good salesman. With one sentence he'd deflected Clay's criticism and turned it into a challenge.

Oh, Clay was the right person, all right. He'd grown up with a hammer in his hand, fixing and building whatever he and his carpenter-by-trade father could find.

He was the right person—but he'd be damned if he'd pay asking price. Only suckers didn't bargain for a better price.

Clay turned to the agent. "Can I think about it and get back to you?"

"Yes, but be aware there's been a lot of interest in the property recently . . ."

Bull shit. Clay had done his homework. He'd looked up the history of the listing online. The house had been on the market for two years and the seller had dropped the price by nearly a hundred thousand dollars total during that time.

He kept that knowledge to himself and let the

agent pretend there were other interested parties.

"I understand. I'll get back to you." Confident there really was no competition and the house would be his—and for twenty thousand below asking, which was what he planned to offer—Clay extended his hand to the agent. "Thanks for your time."

"No problem. I look forward to hearing from you soon."

With a non-committal nod, Clay pivoted and headed out the front door and toward his pick-up truck.

It wasn't until he was behind the wheel and pulling away that he allowed himself to smile. This house was as good as his. No doubt about it.

He navigated to 75 North, heading toward Coronado and his current, hopefully short-term, furnished rental that he'd moved into when he'd retired two months ago.

He'd been looking at properties since then but today's was the first to get him excited. That called for a celebratory drink. He hit a name in his cell's contact list to dial one of his buddies, put the call on speaker and listened to the ringing.

"Hello."

"Hey, Knots. You up for a visit to McP's?"

"Dirtman! You know it. I'm always up for McP's."

Clay smiled at his teammate's willingness to be swayed into day drinking, even during the week. Asher "Knots" Dillon never did say no to an invitation.

"You sure you can get away?" Clay asked. Asher was still on active duty at the base.

"Yeah, sure. Nobody will miss me for an hour. Nothing going on here anyway. I'm basically killing time until my leave starts."

Clay remembered those days, counting the days and hours until leave started, but he wasn't in that world anymore. Now, his whole life was one long leave and today, he intended to take advantage of that and celebrate his new house with a few cocktails.

"Perfect. See you there in about ten?" Clay said.

"Um. Better make it fifteen," Asher corrected.

"You got it. I'll have a bourbon neat waiting for you."

Asher laughed and said, "Well, in that case, I'll be there in ten."

Another check in the pro column for this house—it was less than fifteen minutes away from his and his friends' old stomping ground at Coronado.

It really couldn't be more perfect.

Clay's mind buzzed as he tried to decide how long to wait to call the agent and put in his bid for twenty thousand below asking price.

Three days maybe? Just so he wouldn't look too anxious.

Nah. No way he could wait that long. He was too excited. He wanted in that house as soon as possible so he could start fixing it up. He had a sneaky suspicion he'd be calling tomorrow.

Apparently playing hard to get wasn't his strong suit.

Hitting the accelerator, he sped faster. A dirty martini, served up in a chilled glass with extra olives, awaited him.

CHAPTER TWO

"Tasha. Jane. Can you two come into my office, please?" Jerry had popped his head into Tasha's dressing room and then disappeared just as quickly as he'd come.

Still facing the mirror, Tasha frowned and caught her assistant's gaze in the reflection. "We go on air live in fifteen minutes and he wants to have a meeting now?"

Jane shrugged. "He's the boss."

"Humph." That was all Tasha had to say in response, because even though Jerry was the executive producer of *Good Day, San Diego*, there'd be no show without Tasha.

Viewers tuned in daily to see her.

The Daytime Emmy Award for Best Host of a Lifestyle Program displayed on her mantelpiece had the name *Tasha Jones* engraved on it. Not Jerry Bernstein's.

Tasha took one last glance at herself in the mirror above her make-up table.

Why she bothered looking, she wasn't sure

because however she looked right now was how she was going on air. There'd be no time to change anything now. Not with a command performance in Jerry's office and then the show going live in—she glanced at the time—about thirteen minutes.

She sighed and stood. "Might as well get in there and see what's so important."

Jane nodded and they made their way down the hall together and into Jerry's office.

"Shut the door."

Tasha pivoted to do as Jerry had ordered, without benefit of a *please* or *thank you* from him, she noted.

When she turned back toward the desk, she also took note of the deep furrow between his brows. The man's entire demeanor broadcasted stress.

For the first time since getting this mysterious summons to his office, she stopped being annoyed and began to get worried.

"Jerry, what's wrong?" Tasha lowered herself to perch on the edge of a chair. She had a feeling she might need to be sitting for this.

Next to her, Jane did the same. Tasha resisted the urge to reach out and hold Jane's hand for support— support for herself, not for Jane. Call her selfish, but she was getting scared.

"I wanted you to hear this from me first." Given Jerry's expression and those doom-filled words— nothing good could follow that sentence.

Her pulse whooshed so loud in her ears she barely heard the rest of what he said as he continued, "The network is making the official announcement later today. The show's not being renewed for next season."

When she exhaled the breath she'd been holding

she realized she couldn't get new air into her lungs. For a few panicked seconds it was as if she were underwater, drowning, unable to draw breath.

A few shallow breaths in quick succession convinced her she wasn't going to suffocate, but she might pass out.

"Are you all right?" Jane asked.

Tasha shook her head. She wasn't now and wouldn't be for a long time.

How could she be all right? She'd just bought a condo. She had a huge mortgage on it because she'd expected the show to be renewed.

The ratings were great. She'd just won the Emmy. She'd foreseen no earthly reason why they'd want to cancel a successful show. She still couldn't fathom their motivation.

"Why?" she asked Jerry, appalled to hear her voice sounded as breathless as she felt.

"The network wants to go another direction with their daytime programming."

"What other direction?" she asked, shaking her head, baffled.

He lifted one shoulder. "Harder hitting stories. Political commentary. Big name interviews both from Hollywood and Washington."

She felt the frown form on her brow in spite of the Botox injections she'd gotten at thirty-two years old because she knew she'd better look good on camera for this thankless ageist network that didn't appreciate a successful show when they saw it.

"The viewers like what we do. They love the cooking segments, and cocktail recipes, and the fashion advice, and the celebrity interviews. And the ratings are—"

Jerry's continuous head shaking cut off the rest of Tasha's list of proof that the network was wrong.

"I know, Tash. Everything you're saying is true. Ratings are good but they're stagnant. There's been no growth in viewership for more than two years."

"How can we expect growth? With all the cord cutting and streaming channels out there, no network show is showing growth." In fact, in Tasha's opinion, holding steady was a miracle.

She considered not losing rating points a win in this environment where there were so many other things vying for viewers' attention.

Jerry lifted one shoulder. "Hallmark Network has seen a considerable gain since twenty-sixteen."

Tasha frowned. "Really?"

She considered what he said, which must be true. Jerry might be cold hearted and have horrible timing, but he wasn't an outright liar.

But Hallmark played the opposite of deep political shows. They catered to viewers who wanted light escapism, which was exactly what her show was and what her network wanted to move away from. It only proved her point—the network's new direction was wrong.

She opened her mouth to explain just that when Jerry held up his hand and stopped her words before they left her lips.

"Look, Tash. It was a good show. We had a good run. Five years is longer than most shows make it. But the decision has already been made. They're not going to change their mind no matter what anyone says. Believe me, I tried."

He was already using the past tense when speaking about her show and by association, her career too. It felt like a post-mortem.

She sat, stunned into shocked silence, leaving a long pause in the conversation that neither Jane nor Jerry interrupted.

"When?" she finally asked.

"This season will end as scheduled. Today is the last day of the live shows. As planned, we'll run previously aired content over the summer. The network will launch the new show replacing yours in your time slot in September, beginning the week after Labor Day."

Deep down she hoped ratings sucked, the viewers hated the new show and the network regretted their decision, and she didn't feel at all bad about thinking it.

Even so, none of that would do her any good. If the new show failed nothing would change for her personally.

The news was still going to go out on the wire today that her show hadn't been picked up for another season.

This time of year announcements like that were daily occurrences as networks ironed out their schedules for the upcoming fall season. Shows didn't get picked up all the time, but never *her* show.

It might be foolish to think so, but the cancellation felt like a blemish on her record. A stigma. One that could never be erased.

Blowing out a breath, she steeled herself to move forward—at least through the next hour. After that she could fall apart.

"All right." She stood and smoothed her pencil skirt with her hands.

Turning, she somehow managed to walk out of the

office under her own power even though her legs felt as weak as when she'd been crazy enough to run that half-marathon.

Out in the hall, she looked closely at every face she saw, studying the expression, trying to decide who knew, who didn't.

They were all in the same boat. They too were out of a job. Every one of the crew. *Her* crew. Though not hers anymore. Not after the end of the show today.

That was it then. Next week, instead of going on hiatus and into contract negotiations for what she'd planned on being a nice bump in pay for next season, she'd be unemployed along with everyone else here today.

God, she was so screwed. Her savings weren't going to get her very far. Not after splurging on new furniture to go in her newly purchased condo.

She had to call her agent. She had to start lining up auditions for another job . . .

And she couldn't do any of it until after she got through a one-hour live show, smiling and cheerful on what had to be the worst day of her life.

What the hell had Jerry been thinking springing this on her when she was about to walk on air live?

She added something new to the top of her To Do list—get a freaking drink. She certainly needed one. But unless they happened to be mixing cocktails on the show today, that too would have to wait.

"Five minutes!"

For the first time since getting her dream job, Tasha wasn't happy to hear those words shouted backstage.

But it didn't matter. A studio packed full with a

live audience for today's show waited for her. In five minutes she'd have to go out there and smile and pretend nothing was wrong.

Pretend that she wasn't pissed and upset and jobless and possibly soon to be homeless.

Pretend things were fine. As good as they were before she stepped foot into that office and got the news.

No. Forget all that! She wasn't going to pretend.

The fans loved her. They were and always would be on her side and they deserved the truth. They deserved to know. To find out from her, not from some gossip rag or entertainment show reporter.

That was too impersonal. She had to address this personally. Directly. Now. On air. Straight to the studio audience and the viewers at home.

Nothing much. Just a simple statement that there wouldn't be a season six. That today's would be the last live show. *Ever.*

At that thought her throat tightened and she felt the prick of tears behind her eyes. She ignored the feeling and stalked toward the set.

Jane ran after her. "Are you going to be all right?" she asked.

"Fine." The single strangled word didn't come out sounding as if she were fine. Tasha dared to glance at Jane and saw the concern etched on her features.

Feeling sentimental, Tasha pulled Jane against her in a hug. When she leaned back she saw Jane looked as surprised by the uncharacteristic move as she was herself.

"You're good people, Jane. You'll get another job soon. Probably right away. Someone will scoop you right up." Tasha forced a smile. She'd better get good at doing that—faking smiles.

"You will too. I'm certain." Jane nodded hard, sending her ponytail bobbing.

Tasha let out a snort, wishing she were as sure.

"One minute!" The call brought her back to the obstacle ahead. The show. The last one. Ever.

She drew in a shaky breath and smiled again, ignoring how her eyes had gone blurry. Ignoring too how closely Jane, clearly worried, was watching her, probably wondering if she could pull off this show today. That made two of them.

"Show time," she said as the theme music began to play. She left Jane behind her and strode out onto the set for the final time.

"Good day, San Diego." She delivered the show's opening tag line but couldn't bring herself to go on with business as usual and deliver the next line she was supposed to. The one she'd said every show for five years—*It's going to be a great day.*

"It's *not* such a great day here today, I'm sad to say." Tasha scanned the faces of the crowd as her words sunk in, as one by one they realized she hadn't repeated the usual words.

She continued, "I'm sorry to have to say these words, but today will be the last *Good Day, San Diego* live show. We haven't been renewed for next season."

There were gasps from the audience. A couple of people said aloud, "No."

She dared to glance to the side and saw the looks on the faces of the crew. They were all in this boat together. More like a sinking ship.

Her emotions began to take hold of her.

"The network, in its infinite wisdom, has decided to *change focus.*" Sadness turned to anger and spilled out in her tone as she actually used air quotes to reinforce the words that she still found baffling and ridiculous. "They want *serious* news and politics. Because there's not already enough network and cable news channels running news and politics twenty-four/seven, right?"

Heart pounding, she scanned the audience and saw nods of agreement from those in the crowd.

Encouraged and discouraged all at the same time, Tasha continued, "And you know what? I have to think it's because men are running the network. Men who don't understand or maybe just don't care what a predominantly female audience wants. They're making the decision to change based on what? I certainly don't know. Our ratings are great. We have incredible sponsors. Our viewers are some of the best damn fans in daytime TV."

A cheer and applause rose up making the tears she'd been barely holding back threaten to spill over the rim of her flooded eyes.

"Well, I value your opinion, even if they don't." She was shouting over the applause now and with every one of her words the cheers got louder.

It only reinforced what she knew. She was right. They were wrong. This decision was *wrong*.

"Bunch of fucking dickheads," she mumbled, shaking her head at their stupidity.

Uh, oh. She'd whispered it but, of course, she was wearing a microphone.

Had the audience heard over the noise?

Judging by the looks she was getting from both the audience and the crew, they'd heard.

Oh, well. What were they going to do? Fire her?

Still, she was a professional and the fans had come

here today to be entertained. It was still her job to do that one more time.

"Let's get on with the show, shall we? And since it's my last one, let's make it a great one." With another in what was to become a long hour's worth of forced smiles, Tasha spun and stalked toward her on-stage desk, her legs shaking as she went.

CHAPTER THREE

"Another one, p—please." The visibly intoxicated brunette next to Clay hiccupped as she leaned heavily against the bar rail.

She plunked her empty glass on the bar setting it half on and half off the coaster.

Behind the bar, Raymond paused while drying a glass with a towel and eyed the woman. "You driving?"

"Nope. But thanks for asking. I'm ordering an Uber. *Uber.* That's a funny word. It's fun to say. Uuuuuber."

The bartender, an old retired sailor who'd seen and heard too much in his life, and behind this bar, cocked a brow high. "All right."

He turned to grab a glass to make the drink.

Clay watched as the man mixed something pink and girly in the glass. It reminded him of the Sex on the Beach that one of his teammates always drank in spite of the razzing he took from the guys every time he ordered the damn thing. Though he had to respect his friend for sticking to his guns—or rather his cocktail—no matter what.

The woman tilted her head to look at Clay, frowning as if she'd just noticed him standing there. "Did I cut in front of you?"

Yes, she had, but he was willing to wait. He was a gentleman. Besides, he was in no rush to order his next round since he'd be drinking it solo. Asher had had to head back to base after his one drink.

"It's fine." He waved away her question.

Her blue-eyed gaze dropped down to his flip-flops, then back up, taking in his cargo shorts, his T-shirt and finally, his unshaven face.

Clay hadn't been looked up and down that thoroughly in a long time. Maybe today was going to turn out to be his lucky day all around. He'd found a house. He'd found a woman who was obviously out on the prowl for a man.

"Half day today at work?" she asked.

He frowned and then realized that she was asking why he was dressed like a beach bum at a bar on a Thursday in the middle of the day.

It was still early. Just about fourteen-hundred—make that two p.m. for the civilians of the world, of which Clay had to keep reminding himself he was now one of.

"Better than that." He grinned, answering her question about working a half a day. "No work at all. I got out a couple of months ago."

"Jail." She nodded, her lips pressed tight. "That figures."

"What?" He almost choked on the word.

"I sure can pick 'em," she mumbled, ignoring his shocked question as she shoved a twenty toward the bartender and reached for her drink.

"No. Jesus. Not out of jail. Out of the Navy."

What in the ever-loving hell? Why would she assume when he'd said *out* that he meant he'd just gotten out of jail?

Besides his clearly visible U.S. Navy tattoo on his forearm, in this town you couldn't throw a rock without hitting a sailor. Particularly at this bar. It was owned by a retired SEAL, for fuck's sake. Every second guy in here was probably Navy.

Feeling more insulted the more he thought about her judgmental comment—and that visual once over she'd subjected him to—he couldn't let it go. "What made you think I'd meant jail?"

"No offense." She lifted one shoulder. "I'm a lil' drunk. I had a bad day."

Now it was his turn to nod, accepting her answer without question or comment since it was more than obvious it was the truth. She certainly was drunk. The other part—her supposed bad day—he couldn't know or care less about.

"But you really can't blame me for making assumptions with all that ink on you," she continued, indicating his tattoos with the swirl of one condescending finger.

Things probably would have been fine—he could have walked away without further issue—*if* she'd just kept her pretty little mouth closed and hadn't started in on his tattoos. But instead she'd gone and started talking shit.

Now her gaze swept from the bone frog on his calf, past the U.S. Navy anchor on his forearm and up to the cross tattoo barely visible on his bicep beneath his short sleeves.

That particular one she'd better keep quiet about

or he might just lose his shit. She'd managed to insult him, the SEAL brother he'd lost and memorialized in ink, and his tattoo artist, all in one judgmental glance and a single sentence. A man couldn't let an offense like that stand unaddressed.

He turned to face her head on. "Are you saying my tattoos look like prison ink?"

She lifted a shoulder, grabbing her drink off the bar and sucking hard on the straw.

Her ignorance told him one thing—she wasn't one of those women who hung around bars frequented by SEALs to try to land one for the night. A *frog hog* would have recognized what he was, just from the bone frog on his leg.

Prison ink. He muttered an obscenity beneath his breath, torn between being angry with her over the insult and angry with himself for watching her lips wrap around the straw.

He shouldn't be attracted to a woman this ignorant and bitchy. There must be something wrong with him. Or maybe he just needed to get laid.

Yanking his attention off her mouth, he got back to the subject at hand—her insulting his ink. "I'll have you know these were all done by an award-winning local tattoo artist."

"Really? Hmm. I wouldn't know. I don't have any tattoos." She lifted her shoulder again.

No tattoos, but definitely a stick firmly planted up her ass. Clay let out a snort. "No surprise there."

"What's that supposed to mean?" She swiveled her head to stare at him.

Done with this conversation, Clay didn't pull any punches as he said, "That I can see you're not the type to mar your perfect little body with a lowly tattoo."

"You think I have a perfect body?" Her eyes brightened.

Crap. "No. That's not what I meant."

Even if he had been shamelessly taking advantage of the fact that at six-foot-two he could easily see right down her top. She was on the petite side but it sure didn't affect her big mouth.

He refused to give her the satisfaction of a compliment. "I meant your skin. Not your body." He let out a humph and added, "Vain much?"

There. That should take her down a notch.

What the hell had gotten into him? He was acting like a child, bickering with her instead of keeping his mouth shut.

Another day, he'd be all over this hot chick instead of picking fights with her. But damn, she'd insulted him and his tattoos. Even so, there'd been a time he wouldn't have cared what she said if it meant getting laid.

Damn, he'd gotten old. When had that happened?

Clay knew the answer. Sometime during the twenty years he'd spent serving Uncle Sam.

He drew in a breath and glanced at her—only to find she was checking him out. Not his tattoos. Not his clothes. Him.

As she sucked on her straw, her gaze swept him from head to toe and her expression told him she'd changed her mind and actually liked what she saw.

Apparently she'd gotten over his offensive ink and overly casual attire.

He didn't know her. He didn't like her. But in the grand scheme of things, that didn't matter all that much.

If she were interested, he certainly could be too. He only had to put up with her and her smart mouth for an hour or two. He could definitely come up with a couple of ways to occupy that mouth so she'd shut up.

It was a good plan and good timing. She'd already drained the drink the bartender had made for her at the start of this surreal conversation and Clay hadn't gotten around to ordering his yet.

Time to go.

"Hey, so, um . . ." He realized he didn't even know her name, yet he was already planning all the things he wanted to do to her.

Hmm. He might possibly be thinking with the little head rather than the big one. Oh, well.

"I'm Clay," he said to remedy the situation. "What's your name?"

"Tasha Jones." She'd supplied more than he needed to know. First names only were just fine with him in situations such as this. She said, "Nice to meet you . . . even though you are a rude smart ass."

"*I'm* rude?" His eyes popped wide.

Clay would accept her calling him a smart ass. He'd been told that before, but he was *not* rude. If anyone had been rude during this strange conversation, it had been her.

He opened his mouth to argue, when she continued, "But you're hot. In a rugged, low-class kind of way."

Direct hit, right to the bow. He bit back an obscenity as she lobbed that doozy of an insult at him. She thought he was hot. She was definitely interested. He could get what he wanted if he could just keep his mouth shut.

He pressed his lips together and physically held in the words he wanted to say.

Christ. Did he really want to get laid that badly? He was in the process of changing his mind when her heated gaze dropped down his body again, spending quite a bit of time on his chest before moving down to the bulge beneath his shorts.

His decision was made.

"You, uh, wanna get out of here?" He tipped his head toward the door leading to the street.

"And go where?" She frowned, bringing her gaze up from his crotch to land on his face.

"Your place. Or mine if you want." He shrugged, hoping she'd choose hers. It'd be easier to make a clean getaway when they were done.

He wasn't a sleepover and cuddle kind of guy. He couldn't think of anything worse than the awkward morning after a one-night stand.

"I'll even drive, so you don't have to order a car," he added as extra incentive, remembering her Uber comment.

She looked him up and down again like he was a juicy steak and she was a starving man.

Finally, she reached for the big purse she'd plunked on the bar when she'd paid for her drink. "Okay."

Her answer was a shock. He hadn't actually expected her to say yes.

"Okay?" he repeated, just to make sure.

"Yeah. Come on. Let's go." She turned and took one step toward the door and treated him to the rear view. And what a view it was.

Shit. He was an ass man and she had an amazing one.

He might regret it later but, for better or worse, he was going to do this. He pushed off the bar to catch up with her before she got too far ahead.

The woman stumbled to a stop and glanced back at him with a frown. "Wait. You're not too drunk to drive, are you?"

She wasn't all that drunk herself if she'd thought to ask. That was good. He didn't need to get accused of taking advantage of an intoxicated female.

Besides, that wasn't really his style. He could get plenty of sober women. He didn't need to prey on the drunk ones.

"I'm fine to drive."

With only one martini, ordered over an hour ago, plus the plate of nachos he'd shared with Asher in his belly, he wasn't worried.

When she still eyed him suspiciously, he held up his right hand and said, "I swear. Not drunk."

"Okay. I believe you." She delivered that pronouncement with an exaggerated nod and a burp.

Lovely. With his luck, she'd puke in his truck.

"You feeling okay?" he asked as a preemptive strike against the possible impending vomit he didn't want to clean.

"Yup. I'm fine. As sober as a newly unemployed talk show host should be, I am." She nodded again and swung her arm in an exaggerated sweeping motion toward the door. "Come on."

Clay had no idea what she was talking about and he didn't ask, mainly because he got another good look at the rear view as she wobbled through the exit.

He had to admit, that tight little skirt showed off her lower assets nicely.

Curvy heart-shaped butt. Toned thighs. Wide hips

flaring from a nipped-in waist, which would be the perfect place to anchor his hands while he plunged into her from behind.

Liking that image, he decided on that position for their encounter as he followed her out. Definitely taking this one from behind. Not that she didn't have a face made for staring at—she definitely did in a china doll kind of way—but with it came her mouth, which he'd already seen she liked to run off way too much.

Face down on the pillow should take care of that. Best to keep the discussion to a minimum to avoid any further disagreements.

He decided that was a good game plan as he jumped to catch up with her. He grabbed her arm when she reached the sidewalk and turned right.

"Whoa there. Where you going?" he asked.

She stared at him for a second. "Your car. You're driving. Remember?"

Yes, he remembered. It was a good sign that she did too.

"I'm parked this way." He tipped his head toward the left.

"Oh. Okay." She spun to the left but he kept his hand on her elbow. Safer that way as they crossed the side street.

The sex gods were definitely giving him a run for his money with this one, yet he was still going back to her place.

Was that a testament to her hotness or his horniness?

That was probably one of those chicken and the egg conundrums with no answer. Not worth worrying about.

He clicked the locks and swung open the passenger-side door. She frowned at the seat, nearly chest level with her in spite of her fuck-me high heels, which he intended to enjoy later.

She glanced at him. "I heard men with big trucks have a small penis."

A surprised laugh escaped him. "I assure you that isn't the case."

With Junior already stirring in his shorts, ready to rise to the challenge, he'd enjoy proving that to her the moment they got to her place.

"All right." She reached for the handle in the doorframe and the back of the seat and struggled to get her one foot up. The skirt, narrow and tight and hitting her at mid-thigh, wouldn't let her. She hiked the hem up too far, exposing more of her legs than she probably wanted to, and tried again.

Through it all Clay watched instead of helping her, enjoying the view. Also enjoying watching her vodka-soaked brain reason out how to accomplish her goal in spite of the obstacles.

Maybe he was rude, or at least crude.

He knocked himself out of the trance watching her ass had put him in and boosted her up with a hand on each hip. It was at the same time she used all of her effort to hoist herself up.

The added momentum sent her tumbling face first into the cab of the truck.

He bit his lip to not laugh as she momentarily perched with her head in the driver's seat and her ass high in the air.

It was a good position for a couple of things he wouldn't mind doing with her and it was amusing as hell.

This might turn out to be all right after all.

He was still thinking that as she righted herself. With the tempting view obscured as she sat on it, he moved around to the driver's side and got behind the wheel.

Clay was still thinking it was turning out to be a pretty good afternoon even after he finally got an address out of her and had plugged it into his GPS. She lived across the bridge in San Diego, but he managed to navigate the traffic and find her place.

In fact, he had great hope for a memorable encounter as she led him inside her place, pulled him with her onto a white leather sofa and yanked his head down for a kiss.

No puke in his truck. Straight to the action without any small talk. So far so good.

He reached down and rested one hand on the smooth skin of her thigh. She let her legs fall farther apart and, never one to ignore an invitation, Clay slid his hand up and in between her spread thighs.

As he plunged his tongue between her lips, his hand reached what felt like lace underwear beneath her skirt and he started to get really excited about the possibilities.

She needed to take off the skirt and blouse. Give him a better view of what he'd bet was expensive lingerie because from the looks of her place she liked nice things—when she wasn't drunk that was.

This chick was definitely slumming it with Clay and his *prison ink* now.

Seeing her in nothing but the lingerie with those heels would go far to soothe his bruised ego and getting laid would go a long way to get him over her insults.

He might even be able to laugh about this one day. It would at least make a good story to tell the guys.

With his main goal in mind, he was victorious in the battle against her tight skirt and finally wiggled it up enough he could get to the spot between her legs that made her moan.

He slipped two fingers inside her, stroking as he circled her with his thumb. She spread her legs wider.

Her moans had him thinking things were progressing nicely toward his end goal. When her orgasm broke, he was sure of it—this was going to be one hell of a night.

She broke the kiss, breathing heavily as he continued to work her, pushing her past the end of her orgasm.

He was ready to rip his pants off and enjoy her hot core with his cock rather than his hand when he felt it . . . her body relax, sagging limp against the cushions.

Then he heard it . . . the soft tell tale deep breathing of a woman asleep—or possibly passed out.

Crap.

Resigned, Clay eased his hand out from beneath her skirt and stood.

It looked like the only thing he was getting today was that good story to tell his teammates. Though, on second thought, he didn't even have that since there was no way in hell he'd admit to the guys a woman had fallen asleep while his hand was up her skirt.

They'd tease him about that until the day he died. It could even earn him yet another nickname. Something far less flattering than his current *Dirtman*. Something like Sandman because he'd put her to sleep during foreplay.

Yeah, no. This story was going with him to the

grave.

He sighed.

The A/C was pumping icy air into the room—proving the woman didn't worry about conserving power and saving the world or reducing her carbon footprint or whatever the hell the politically correct saying was nowadays.

He glanced down at her, sound asleep and noticed the goose bumps rising on her skin.

With a scowl, he grabbed the white throw that was folded on the arm of the sofa. He flipped it open and laid it over her, covering the tempting legs he'd almost made it between and those luscious tits he would have enjoyed immensely.

He'd consider not letting her freeze while she was passed out his good deed for the day, done without any reward or hope of one.

No thanks. No loving. He might as well have been her Uber driver except he didn't even get paid for the ride home.

Clay let himself out of her apartment, making sure the door was locked before he pulled it shut behind him.

Now that he wasn't getting sex, he realized he was starving. His mind turned to a nice juicy bone-in rib-eye steak, seared on the outside and bloody in the middle.

Yeah, that would hit the spot. It would be almost as good as sex.

Almost . . .

CHAPTER FOUR

Realization came slowly.

At first everything was okay—good even as Tasha clawed her way up from sleep and into consciousness.

Then she began to notice things. Bad things. The fuzzy feel of her teeth. The dull headache. The nausea and dizziness as she opened her eyes. The fact she was on the sofa and fully dressed in the clothes she'd worn to work.

Hangover.

The word flew into her brain. It made perfect sense. It had been a while since she'd been hung over but she remembered well the feeling.

Her memory was the last thing to return. She remembered she was no longer employed. Might never be employed again after her on-air meltdown.

No wonder she'd gotten drunk at the bar—

Holy shit! The bar. The guy. She'd brought him home.

She sat up too fast and paid the price in pain and queasiness.

Where was he? Was he still here? Had they—?

Eyes wide, she reached down beneath the blanket covering her. Her skirt was hiked way up, almost around her hips. Not a good sign. Her underwear were still on but that didn't mean much.

Jesus. Did they even use a condom? That man could be carrying all sorts of diseases.

Her stomach churned and it wasn't all from the hangover.

Bringing home a stranger. Having sex with him. Apparently she made very bad decisions when she drank too much.

No more getting drunk ever.

Glancing around she spotted her purse. At least that had made it home with her. She sat upright and groaned. Sudden movements were proving to be a bad idea.

She shuffled slowly over to the table where she'd dumped her bag. Inside she found her wallet and credit cards along with a couple of bills. A hell of a lot less than she'd gone to the bar with, though most likely she'd drunk her cash away.

Her car keys were inside her purse as well. She remembered climbing into a huge high truck. He must have driven her home—whoever *he* was—so her car had to still be parked at the bar—she hoped.

She'd have to get over there and pick it up— maybe later when she could move without fear of vomiting.

The muffled sound of her cell phone ringing caught her attention.

Was that her one-night stand from last night calling her for a booty call? That would be just her luck. She couldn't get guys she actually liked and could picture a future with to call her back after a first date, but the one she couldn't remember having drunken sex with would totally call her the next day.

Lovely. He must really be a loser. A desperate loser. Just like she was.

A bit of rummaging—and moaning because damn her head hurt—and she finally made hand-to-cell contact inside the cavernous interior of her bag.

Wondering when she'd set the ringtone so damn loud, she pulled it out and groaned when she read the name on the display.

Milly.

Her agent.

Uh, oh.

Sitting and flopping back against the sofa's cushions, Tasha punched the screen and answered the call. "Hello?"

"Have you been online yet today?" Tasha's agent had dispensed with the greeting and gotten right down to the point.

Since her brain was running a little slow, she couldn't figure out why Milly would care if she'd had time to log into Instagram today or not. "Um, no. Why?"

"Why don't you go ahead and look for yourself. I'll wait." Her tone told her this wasn't a good thing. It had to be about what she'd said on air yesterday.

"Which site?" she asked.

Milly laughed. "Pick one. Instagram. YouTube. Twitter. Facebook. You're everywhere. Gifs. Memes. Even a remixed video set to music. Congratulations, Tasha, you've gone viral."

After yesterday's show, Tasha had a feeling that wasn't a good thing. She'd run out of the studio the minute they'd yelled it was a wrap so she didn't have to face Jerry.

She'd never considered the video of her on-air meltdown would go viral.

But everything she'd said had only been the truth. How could people fault her for that?

Hoisting herself off the sofa again, she stood motionless for a second as the room swung, before she moved to the desk and sank into the chair.

Luckily the laptop was in sleep mode, so all she had to do was flip open the lid and it sprang to life. There was her browser, open to the last page she'd been on yesterday before work when she'd still had a job.

"Just search 'talk show host loses it on air' and it should come right up," Milly told her.

Uh oh. That was definitely not a good thing.

The search results told Tasha that Milly hadn't been exaggerating. She'd indeed gone viral. That was one thing to check off her bucket list.

She leaned closer and selected one. It was a gif of her saying *dickheads* over and over again in an eternal loop.

The next search result was a meme. It had Tasha's heart clenching as she read it. "I don't always lose my shit on TV, but when I do, I do it with a career-ending bang."

Had that two minutes on air in the beginning of yesterday's show ended her career?

It might well have. Who would want to hire a host who went off on-air, criticizing her own network? No one.

Tasha was shaking, scared and angry both, when she swallowed hard and said, "Milly, the bastard told me ten minutes before I had to go on the air for the last live show ever."

"Well, at least you restrained yourself and didn't actually call Jerry a bastard on-air too. You limited your insults to only calling the network executives dickheads who are too stupid or chauvinistic to care what women want."

"I didn't call them stupid—did I?" Crap. She'd better watch the video.

"Not in so many words, no. But the subtext was there. Loud and clear. And the entertainment reporters didn't miss it. There are already plenty of posts and articles up online about your little meltdown. With this momentum, I expect it might even make prime time. You might want to watch *Entertainment Tonight* this evening."

Tasha groaned. That had always been her dream, for her local show to be big enough to get covered by the national prime time entertainment shows. But not like this.

She swallowed and forced herself to address the issue that had her gripped in fear. "Am I done, Milly? Have I ruined any chance of a career?"

Her agent's pause, however short, had Tasha's hopes plummeting. Finally, Milly said, "I honestly don't know."

"Oh." That single word was all she could manage as the tears began to spill.

Milly drew in an audible breath. "I did have something come across my desk recently. I didn't tell you about it because—well, you had a job then. I'm not sure if you'd be interested—"

"I'm interested." Tasha sat up a little straighter.

"Wait. Let me finish. It's not network. It's cable."

Tasha gripped the cell tighter, clinging to this new

hope. "I don't care."

"It's a home renovation show."

"That's fine. I can do that."

"Oh, can you?" Milly let out a laugh. "When's the last time you held a hammer in your hand?"

"Just last week." Okay, the hammer was pink and had come in a leopard print toolbox she'd bought because it was cute, but the fact remained she owned tools and she could use them.

"And what did you do with it?" Milly's skepticism was clear in her tone.

She hesitated, but had to admit, "When I couldn't crack the shell of my take-out King Crab Legs, I used my hammer."

"That's not exactly the same as renovating," Milly said.

"I can learn. Besides, wouldn't there be a real carpenter on the show and I'd be more like the host?" It would be just like *Good Day, San Diego*. She never actually did the cooking herself. The guest chef did and she just stood next to them and talked.

"I don't know all the details for the show but I'll find out."

"And you'll put my name in for the job?" Tasha resisted the urge to cross her fingers for luck.

Again Milly paused, before saying, "Yes, I'll put your name in. But, Tasha, you need to toe the line. No comments to the media. No posting on social. No responding to anything anyone posts about you. Got it?"

"You don't think I should at least post an apology?"

"No! Just leave it be. You said it. It's out there. There's no taking it back. It doesn't matter what you say now, the haters are gonna hate and your supporters will continue to love you. Let the story die, the sooner the better. Don't feed into it. Someone will do something else stupid soon enough and you'll be completely forgotten."

Completely forgotten.

Didn't Milly know that was Tasha's worst fear?

CHAPTER FIVE

Clay picked up his cell—and then put it down again for what had to be the twentieth time that morning.

Antsy, he glanced around the one bedroom apartment he rented, looking for something to take his mind off wanting to call the real estate agent.

A single window in the living area looked out at a narrow piece of grass and the house next door that blocked his sunlight, as well as any view.

There wasn't a whole hell of a lot to do within the four walls. No wonder he was going stir crazy.

On a gorgeous day like today, he wanted to be outside, not indoors watching some show he could care less about. He wanted to be outside in his own yard, looking out at his own little piece of beach.

Fuck it. He wanted that house. He didn't care if it hadn't even been twenty-four hours since he'd seen it or that calling would make him seem too eager and willing to pay asking price.

Since he'd cued it up this morning before he talked himself out of calling, the number was right there in his cell when he unlocked the screen.

He hit the number and, breathing a little faster, waited as he listened to the ringing.

"Russell Ramirez speaking."

"Hey, it's Clay Hagan. You showed me the Imperial Beach property yesterday."

"Yes, of course I remember. Good morning."

"Good morning. So, uh, I've thought about it and even though the house does need a lot of work, I think I'd like to put in an offer."

"Excellent, I'm glad you called before it's too late."

Clay rolled his eyes. These agents, always trying to create a sense of urgency by pretending there were other interested parties when in reality there weren't. If there had been, the property wouldn't have sat on the market for two years.

Refusing to play this game, Clay cut right to the chase and said, "So I'd like to offer twenty thousand below asking price."

"All right. But I feel I need to tell you that there's another bid currently in and being considered by the seller."

Clay didn't like the sound of that. "And?" he asked.

Ramirez paused and finally said, "Under asking is not likely to be competitive in this situation."

That revelation knocked the wind right out of Clay's lungs.

There was another bid. He could lose this house.

"Would you like to raise your bid, Mr. Hagan, or would you like me to present it to the seller for twenty under asking?"

In a position he did not like being in, Clay had to trust this man's integrity, even if Ramirez did stand to gain financially on this transaction.

"How much more do you suggest I offer?" he asked, afraid of the answer.

"That's completely up to you, of course."

Clay sighed at the man's evasiveness. "So, like, asking price?"

"Um . . ." Ramirez hesitated.

Crap. Sucking it up, even as much as it hurt, Clay said, "Or five-thousand over asking?"

"I believe that would be a nice strong offer."

Ouch. Twenty-five thousand more than he'd hoped to spend. That hurt. He sucked in air through his teeth. There was nothing to be done about it. He wanted this house.

"All right, let's go with that then," Clay agreed, trying and failing at calculating in his head what that would do to the down payment amount and his savings account balance and his monthly mortgage payments.

"Great. I'll present that number to the seller right away and get back to you."

"Thanks." His mood had deflated exponentially since he'd picked up the cell. He had to know if it was going to fall any further. "Um, Ramirez, do you think I have any chance of getting it?"

If this became a bidding war and he was up against some real estate developer with tons of financial resources, Clay knew he'd lose. He had limited savings, all from pinching pennies while in the Navy with an eye toward a comfortable retirement. He didn't want to take on a huge mortgage at this point in his life.

"I think you're in a very competitive position. You're a veteran. Local. Preapproved for a mortgage.

You plan to live there yourself rather than flip it. I'll make sure the seller knows. I think that will work in your favor."

How had this guy learned all that about him in the few short hours they'd spent together looking at properties, during which Clay had done his best to not give too much away?

Ramirez was better at his job than he'd given him credit for. And if he really was going to put in a good word for him with the seller, Clay owed the man more than the bad attitude he'd been giving him.

"Thank you. I appreciate it." Clay couldn't muster optimism, but he was slightly less deflated than he had been a moment ago.

The agent seemed to be on his side. That had to be better than having no one in his corner.

"You're welcome. I'll present this right away and get back to you when I have an acceptance or a counter offer."

A counter offer. Christ. That would mean more money. He was going to have to really sit down and crunch some numbers and see what this was going to do to his finances.

Drawing in a breath, Clay resigned himself to the reality of this situation and said, "All right. Thanks."

He disconnected the call, beating himself up mentally. He should have put in a bid on the spot. Right there while standing in the house. Instead he'd been playing games, waiting to make an offer. That decision could cost him the property. He'd been so stupid!

Now he really couldn't sit inside the apartment. He had to get out and expend some of this energy or the waiting might kill him.

He stalked to the bedroom to change into his running clothes.

Hell, maybe he'd run to the bar and take advantage of the one perk this rental provided—proximity to his favorite drinking establishment.

It was a bit too early to have his usual dirty martini, even for him, but he could definitely drown his sorrows with a nice cold beer. It wouldn't help the seller's decision come any faster, or in his favor, but it would certainly help his frame of mind.

CHAPTER SIX

"What are you doing right now?" Milly asked, again without bothering to say hello after Tasha had answered the call.

"Right now?" Tasha glanced down at herself. She couldn't admit she was still wearing the same clothes from yesterday that she'd woken up in.

Was it still a walk of shame if you were in your own home? She didn't know, but she wasn't going to confess to her agent that she was too depressed to get off the sofa and put on different clothes.

She'd been lucky she'd had the energy to shuffle to the kitchen and get coffee. Thank God for one-step brewing, even if all those plastic single-use pods were going to destroy the environment one day.

"Yes, right now." Milly was still waiting for an answer.

Since Tasha didn't have one for her she said, "Nothing. Why?"

"Can you meet with the producer?"

"What?" Tasha sat up, that news giving her more energy than the caffeine had.

"The reality show I told you about. The producer is there to take another look at a property they're bidding on for the show. Imperial Beach, she said. That's not too far from you, right? I googled it and it looked fairly close."

Milly being in Los Angeles didn't know but Tasha sure did. That was damn close to San Diego. It would be perfect. Depending on traffic, her set could be less than half an hour down the road . . . if she got this job.

"Yes, I can meet. When? Where?"

"You tell me. They're heading to the house now. They figure they'll be there for at least half an hour, taking pictures and measurements and stuff. They're not local so they don't know the restaurants. She asked where you'd like to meet."

The one place Tasha could think of with her foggy hung over brain, blurred even more now with excitement, was the bar where she'd abandoned her car yesterday.

She had to get there today anyway to retrieve her vehicle. And it was a cool place with a ton of local history and Navy stuff on display.

"How about McP's Irish Pub in Coronado? It's probably halfway between the property and me. I'll text you the exact address." She didn't have time to do much to get ready, but she could jump in the shower, throw on some make-up and a casual dress, order an Uber and get over there by the time the producer had looked at the property and driven to the bar. "I can be there in an hour."

"Perfect. Text me that address and I'll call her right away."

Oh my God. Her career wasn't dead. She hadn't

killed it. They wanted to meet her. Fate was giving her another chance and she wasn't about to squander it.

Tasha made it to McP's in forty-eight minutes flat. She knew because she'd watched the time ticking away on her cell phone as she sat in the back of the car.

She walked into the dim interior, blinded from the sunlight because her sunglasses were in her car, which was, of course, still parked here where she'd left it yesterday. She probably had a parking ticket by now but she didn't take the time to check. Meeting the producers and getting this job was more important than worrying about any fine.

As the sun spots before her eyes subsided, she made her way across the dim space and to the man behind the bar.

"Hey, I'm meeting a couple of people here. Will we be able to get a table outside when they arrive?"

The bartender glanced through the back door and said, "Doesn't look too crowded. Shouldn't be a problem."

"Great. Thanks. Um, can I have a seltzer with lime while I wait?"

"Sure."

As the bartender went off to get her soda, Tasha turned and stopped dead. A memory hit her when she saw first the muscular forearm of the hand holding the beer, then the bicep and the tattoos decorating both.

When she finally felt brave enough to raise her gaze to his face, she knew what she'd find.

"You," she breathed.

Of all the bars in all the world, her drunken one-night stand had to be here, now, the morning after she'd slept with him and didn't remember it.

"Me." He smiled, looking cocky.

Of course he was full of himself. He'd gotten laid last night. Why wouldn't he be pleased?

"Here you go." The bartender delivering her seltzer knocked her out of her shocked silence.

"Thanks." She turned to take it, which had the added benefit of her not having to face *him*, her drunken mistake.

Though at least she hadn't been wearing beer goggles at the time. He was still hot, even by the sober light of day.

Tall, dark and handsome with muscles like a stone wall and a smile that could melt a woman's heart. And those green and gold-flecked eyes . . . she cut her gaze sideways to get another look and saw him still smirking at her.

Yanking her gaze back to the glass in front of her, she vowed not to make the mistake of trying to sneak another look again.

Best to let this whole mistake die without further discussion. She certainly wasn't about to repeat it. She wasn't drinking today. She'd already decided that.

Besides, she had the meeting with the producer. She needed to keep her wits about her for that. Prove that she wasn't the lunatic social media was making her out to be.

And more importantly, the more she thought about this man and yesterday, the more she remembered. If her drunken memories could be trusted, he'd been a bit of an ass.

A cute ass, but an ass nonetheless. There was no room in her dating life for that kind of man.

As she concentrated overly hard on not looking at

him, she was happy when his cell phone rang and he turned and moved farther down the bar to answer it.

Things were going her way. Finally.

Yesterday had just been a bad day all around, but not today. Today was turning out to be the polar opposite, proving that good things did happen to good people.

She smiled. She was going to be all right. She could feel it.

CHAPTER SEVEN

When Clay's phone rang he recognized the real estate agent's number. Turning away from the woman, his very own ghost of hook-ups past, he answered, "Ramirez."

"Yes. Hello, Mr. Hagan. I have news."

"Go ahead." Clay braced himself for this news, which had better be good since he and his bank account couldn't afford any more bad.

"The other bidders countered with an amount above your bid. The seller is giving you the opportunity to raise your offer."

Fuck. Clay mouthed the obscenity but managed to not say it aloud.

"What would you like me to do?" the agent asked.

Closing his eyes, Clay drew in a breath and ignored how much it hurt him to say, "Would matching their current bid do any good?"

"You can. Of course, the other buyer might just go higher."

God, he hated this whole game. Hated it with every fiber of his being. Give him a clear enemy he could see and he'd go at him head-on and full force. But this—this negotiating through a third party against an unknown opponent might be enough to drive him insane.

He blew out a breath. "Go seven thousand over my prior bid."

"Okay. I think that's a good move. I'll present it to the seller and get back to you."

"Yeah. Thanks." As fast as his money was pouring out of his savings account with each and every phone call from Ramirez, Clay hoped the next call didn't come quite as fast as the last. Unless it was good news, of course.

He was beginning to think good news would never come and this whole house dream of his was just that—a dream.

More like a lost cause.

Meanwhile, just slightly down the bar, his almost one-night stand had been joined by two other women.

Clay sighed. He missed the good old days when this place was just a dive, frequented mainly by squids and frogmen. Back when he'd been fresh out of BUD/S and he'd come to McP's with the whole team as newly minted SEALs.

That was long ago, before the tour trolley began dropping off a steady stream of visitors directly in front.

Nowadays when he came in he was more likely to see tourists rather than frogman. There was even a website with an online store that sold McP's-branded SEAL T-shirts.

Just like everything else in the world, his favorite haunt had gone commercial.

Today instead of sailors, bellied up to the bar were three dressed-up city women, one of whom he knew couldn't hold her liquor.

Clay shook his head, hating change. Hating the chattering of these women encroaching upon his territory even more.

He could sure use a martini, but instead Clay waited for Raymond to finish what he was busy doing so he could order one more beer. He'd have to ask for a chaser of water too so he didn't dehydrate since after this next beer, he intended to sprint all the way back to his apartment for a shower.

Besides, he couldn't get plastered even if it might ease the pain of the rising cost of this house. He needed his wits about him today. Now that his renovation fund was being rapidly depleted in this ridiculous bidding war, he'd have to get online and start researching. Make a list of what he'd need for the renovation and then compare prices of big ticket items like the building materials and tools he'd need.

Traveling so much with the team meant he hadn't collected a whole lot of personal stuff. It also meant he'd have to buy a lot of it new now.

The way the negotiations had been going, he only hoped he had any money left to buy anything at all after the down payment and closing costs, not to mention the monthly mortgage payments slowly creeping up along with the purchase price.

Christ, was he going to have to get a job? He'd planned to live on his retirement pay and his savings. But now—

"Oh my God! That house is *amazing*." Tipsy Tasha's overly loud and excited exclamation drew Clay's attention back to her and her two companions.

"It really is. And a steal too. To get a house on the beach for that amount . . ." The woman shook her head. "I couldn't believe it when I saw the listing. And it needs work, which is perfect because that's the whole point of the show, right?"

"Exactly." Tasha nodded. "I just love the architecture too. It has character. You can definitely tell it's older."

The third woman said, "It was built in the 1950s. That was one of the other things that drew us to it besides the price and the fact it's beach-front. It's quirky, you know? Even the color has personality. We didn't want another cookie cutter house."

"Right!" Tasha agreed. "I love the turquoise blue. So fun."

As he listened, his frown deepened. Every comment the three women had made could be said about his house.

His was blue and from the fifties. On the beach and in need of work. And a great price—or at least it had been. That was rapidly changing.

But it couldn't be the same house. That would be crazy. Although it was only a twelve-minute drive from here with no traffic. A buyer could conceivably stop by for a drink on the way back from a showing. He had done exactly that.

Tasha was still holding up the cell phone the other woman had handed her. He moved slightly so he could glance over her shoulder and—

Mother fucker!

There it was in living color in the photo on the cell phone—his house.

"That's my house." In his shock, he said it aloud, whether he'd meant to or not.

One of the women glanced up at him, looking surprised. "You're the seller?"

"No, I'm the other buyer you keep outbidding." He scowled, trying not to tell them exactly what he thought of their swooping in and trying to steal his purchase.

Tasha turned to face him. "Then it's not your house, is it? If they bid higher, and the seller accepted their offer over yours, then it's *their* house."

Clay stood to his full height and took a step forward, closing in on Tasha, knowing full well how intimidating he could be when looming over someone smaller.

He'd backed men far larger than her into corners with his glare alone.

"Well, Miss Know-It-All, the seller hasn't accepted their offer. So it's nobody's house yet."

"I have no doubt they can outbid any amount *you* can come up with." Her gaze dropped down his body, as it had the night before when she'd been sizing him up.

Today, dressed in a sweaty T-shirt featuring a martini glass and the words *I like it dirty*, with PT shorts and running shoes, he probably looked even worse than yesterday in her eyes.

His brows slammed down over his eyes in an angry frown. "What the fuck is that supposed to mean?"

"Nothing." She smirked and lifted one bare shoulder, ignoring he'd leaned in even closer to glare at her.

Normally, he'd enjoy that she wore a barely-there sundress with plenty of cleavage showing. Today, his blood pressure skyrocketed instead. "You know nothing about me," he spat.

"And you know nothing about me, in spite of . . . *whatever* happened." Her expression turned insecure, questioning, almost fearful.

His mouth dropped open in realization. "Oh my God. You can't remember last night, can you?"

She must have been drunker than he'd thought to black out and not remember if she had sex with him or not—which made him even more grateful it was *not.*

He didn't need any accusations flying around that he'd taken advantage of her. She seemed just the type to regret things the morning after and cry foul.

Her eyes widened, before she shot a quick glance at her companions and then turned to glare a warning at him.

A smile he couldn't control bowed his lips. She must think they did have sex last night and she didn't want her home-stealing friends to know she'd gone home with someone as lowly as she apparently thought he was.

This new development he could work with.

"Maybe if you convinced your friends over there to back off and I were to get my house, I could walk away from this whole situation without another word. But if I don't get my house . . ." He lifted one shoulder and delivered a pointed glance at Tasha's two friends, who were watching the discussion with undisguised interest.

With her eyeballs in danger of popping out of her head, she hissed in a breath. "You wouldn't stoop that low."

She'd kept her voice low so only he would hear. Yup, she definitely didn't want these two other women to know about last night. How amusing.

"Wouldn't I?" He cocked up a brow.

She blew out a loud breath, looking torn between anger and panic.

He knew the feeling. He felt the exact same way at the prospect of losing his house to these people—whoever they were.

"Might I make a suggestion?"

Clay raised his gaze to the tall blonde whose name and purpose for being here—besides to steal his house—he didn't know.

"And who are you?" he asked.

"I'm the person who might be able to give you exactly what you want."

He crossed his arms and scoffed at her overly dramatic comment. He'd bet his next retirement check that she was from Hollywood. She had the look and sound about her.

"Oh my God. He's absolutely perfect." The brunette standing next to the blonde evaluated Clay with a smile.

"Right? Both of them. They're perfect together. The chemistry is off the charts." Blondie's confusing reply to her sidekick's equally baffling comment had Clay frowning.

"Perfect for what? What are you talking about?" A single glance at Tasha told Clay she might know a bit more than he did about what was happening, but she looked no happier about it than he was. "Do you know what's going on?" he asked her.

She raised her gaze to him. "I think I can guess."

Annoyed, he widened his eyes. "Does someone want to fill me in?"

"I'd love to. Can we sit?" Blondie asked.

"You buying?" he asked.

She nodded with a smile. "Of course."

Still not moving, he decided to push a bit further, since she was being so agreeable. "You going to back off my house?" he asked.

She smiled wider. "That will depend on you."

What the fuck was happening? Out of options and still confused, Clay pushed off the bar.

"All right. Fine." He glanced at the bartender. "Raymond, we're sitting down. Can you send over another beer for me and put my last one on their tab?" He tipped his head toward the woman willing to foot the expense for his drinking just to talk to him. He wasn't going to argue.

Raymond nodded. "You got it, Dirtman."

It was good to be a regular.

"Thanks, man." Clay turned and made his way outside to the tables in the enclosed courtyard.

Once seated, he had every intention of ordering himself a nice platter of wings too, on them. It was the least he deserved since they were going to cost him tens of thousands of dollars more by bidding up the price of the house . . . if they ever backed off and let him have it at all.

He supposed he'd find out either way soon enough. In the meantime, he was going to order whatever the hell he wanted in the process and they'd be paying for it all.

Ha! He felt better already. And if he got his house back from the thieves who'd tried to steal it out from under him, and didn't have to go any higher than he had already on the price, he'd be a slightly poorer, but happy man.

CHAPTER EIGHT

Tasha knew the plan for the yet to be named home improvement reality show was to have two hosts. A female—that would be her, hopefully—and a male. Only she'd assumed her male counterpart would be a professional carpenter or something like that. Not the Neanderthal from the bar she'd taken home while she'd been drunk.

But from the comments the producers had made, and their interest in talking more with him, they were considering him.

What were they thinking?

Sure he had Popeye forearms and was built like a brick wall—or a man who could build a brick wall with his own two hands—but still.

Ugh. She had to put a stop to this. She'd have to find someone better. There had to be a hot builder out there somewhere. She'd troll every construction site in the state looking for him if she had to. Anybody would be better than—*him*.

Crap, she couldn't even remember his name, if she'd ever known it. How drunk had she been last night anyway?

The answer to that question was clear in her lack of memories—*very* drunk.

Tasha wouldn't make that mistake again.

"So," Joanne, blonde and beautiful and the head of production, settled onto one of the high stools at the table outside. "Tasha, would you like to make the introductions?"

Uh oh. Her eyes widened. "Um."

"Yes, Tasha, introduce me to your friends." His smirk told her he suspected she didn't remember his name.

She turned toward him and forced a saccharin smile. "You feel free to introduce yourself. I know you like to be in charge."

He cocked up one brow to match the crooked smile that quirked up one corner of his mouth. "You're right. I do like to be in control. I didn't think you'd remembered *that* part about our time together. I'm glad you do, though."

The cocky, annoyingly handsome and over the top manly man winked at her. Tasha was torn by the turmoil of hormones and emotions that one ridiculous—and ridiculously effective—wink caused within her.

She didn't know whether she wanted to lift her skirt so this nameless man could show her what she couldn't remember about her night with him or if she wanted to crawl under the table and die of embarrassment.

When she glanced at the women from the production company, she saw they were riveted, their full attention on the surreal interaction between her and her forgotten and regrettable one-night stand.

He was no help. Instead of being a gentleman—or at least a man—and introducing himself, instead he sat there looking amused at Tasha's expense.

She let out an annoyed huff.

Finally, the producer took control of the situation and ended the agony of the eternally long awkward silence. She stood and extended one hand toward the caveman. "I'm Joanne Rossi, executive producer and head of development for New Millennia Media."

He dropped his gaze to her hand before finally extending his own for a brief shake. "Clay."

Clay. Tasha turned the name over in her mind and found it felt kind of familiar.

That made her feel moderately better. She'd at least known the name of the obnoxious but hot man she'd taken home and had forgettable sex with while in a drunken stupor.

Joanne paused but it became apparent that no further information was forthcoming from the man. Finally, she said, "Nice to meet you, Clay. This is Maria Hortez, our director for this project."

His gaze moved to the director. "What project?"

"A renovation project on your house, *if* we can come to an agreement." Joanne smiled.

Clay leaned back as the waiter came to deliver his beer, but not before Tasha saw him react to the producer's use of the words *your house*.

It was obvious Joanne was a master negotiator, like most in her position were. She knew just how to manipulate him.

On the other hand, Clay proved he wasn't without skills of his own as he reached for the long neck bottle and pressed it to his lips in an unhurried motion. The smug move looked calculated, to prove he was in control and that they could all wait for him to be ready to continue.

Setting down the bottle, he finally said, "I'm listening."

Damn, the man was good. The production company had the power and the money and, as far as she knew, the top bid on the house he obviously wanted. But now that he had his game face on, Tasha would never have guessed how much was on the line for Clay in this negotiation.

In seemed of the three parties represented here, she was the only one without bargaining skills. She hated that every thought and emotion showed on her face—when it wasn't spewing out of her mouth at the most inopportune time.

She hated that Clay could look so calm and cool when her heart pounded until she felt light-headed as fear that she wouldn't get this job gripped her.

On the other hand, a feeling of dread overwhelmed her, dismay that she *would* get the job and that her co-star would be Mr. Obnoxious, her one-night stand.

Hate it or not, she'd do it. She'd do the show even if they chose this insufferable beast of a man to be her co-host.

Tasha knew even without her agent's warning that after her viral public meltdown and the show's cancellation this could be her one chance to salvage her on-air career.

Milly should be here for this. This is what Tasha paid her for.

It was too late now.

When they'd set up this meeting it wasn't meant to be a negotiation. Just a quick, casual, get to know you kind of thing. Clay's presence had turned it into something else entirely.

Now it felt like they were all playing hardball and the final score would determine her future. It was yet another reason to resent Clay, as if she needed another one.

"We're producing a home renovation reality show—" Joanne began, only to be interrupted by Clay's snort.

When she paused and lifted a single brow in silent question, Clay said, "There's no *reality* about any of those shows."

"Well, I can assure you one thing will be real and that will be that we're using the bungalow in Imperial Beach. Whether or not *your* name is on the deed or *ours* is when we finish production is what we're discussing now."

That sobered him fast enough.

When he remained quiet, Joanne continued, "The concept is to show the renovation from start to finish."

"There's too many of those shows on TV already. What's going to make this one different? And how does any of this involve me? You think I'm gonna buy it from you after you're done screwing it up?"

"Ah, but that's the part where you come in. You'll be the one doing the renovating."

He frowned. "What do you mean? You're going to hire me to be the contractor?"

"In a way." Maria smiled.

Clay was confused. Tasha could tell that much from his expression.

He wasn't going to grasp what was happening the way Joanne and Maria were dancing around the subject. Tasha might dislike this man, but she hated this long drawn-out guessing game more.

Time to end it. "They want you to be one of the two on-air hosts for the reality show. You'd do the work on camera."

His eyes popped wide before they narrowed. She could see the pieces fall into place in his mind, like watching a chimp trying to figure out how to get a banana out of a box.

He swung his gaze from Tasha to Joanne. "And in exchange you step away from the purchase and I can buy the house?"

She nodded.

"You already drove the price up tens of thousands of dollars above what I initially offered. The price I would have gotten it for if you weren't in the picture since it sat on the market for two years before you came around." He folded his arms and leveled his gaze on her. "What about that financial hardship you caused me? Will I be compensated for that?"

Joanne's lips twisted in what looked like more of a forced than a genuine smile. Tasha had been in this business long enough to know the difference. "You will be compensated. Yes."

"And who has the final say regarding the design choices? Because I don't want you messing up my house since I'm the one who's going to be living in it."

"You can make the final choices. Of course," Joanne said.

Clay pressed his lips together. "The deed is in my name and mine alone?"

"Your name alone *if* all of the conditions laid out in the contract between us are met."

"Then I think we have a deal." Grinning, he reached for the beer again.

Joanne's smile was victorious now. "I think we do. I'll have my lawyer send over a contract for your participation in the show. Once you sign it, we'll tell the real estate agent we're withdrawing our latest offer on the house."

It seemed like a done deal. Sign on the line. Everyone walks away happy. Simple. But Tasha knew better.

These deals, and the accompanying contracts, were never simple. This man was swimming with the sharks, dealing with Joanne and her lawyers. Judging by his smug look of satisfaction, he had no idea who he was up against.

Tasha shouldn't care, but she had to. If all went well, she'd be right there alongside him for the duration of this show and she had a feeling when Clay was unhappy, he made everyone around him miserable.

Joanne slid her business card across the table to him. "Email your information to my office for the contract. We'll messenger it over by tomorrow morning."

"I look forward to it." He stood. "Thanks for the beer."

He looked like he'd gotten everything he'd come for and more. So happy, he even spared a moderately pleasant tip of his head toward Tasha on his way out.

Once he'd gone, Tasha turned her attention back to Joanne and Maria.

"Well, that was easy," Maria said.

"Yes, it was. Now, for you." Joanne leveled her gaze on Tasha.

"Me?" Tasha asked.

Joanne cocked up a brow. "Yes, you. You know as much as we do that he's only half of the equation."

"Exactly. So what's the history between you two, anyway?" Maria asked.

"Um, not much. I actually only met him yesterday." Tasha shrugged as if that were all and tried to evaluate if they believed it.

By the twitch of their lips, she hadn't convinced them completely, but she didn't care. They wanted her for this show. She was the other half of the equation. Whatever was between her and Clay—sex, hate, hate sex—the producers liked it.

"So let's get down to business." Joanne's negotiating smile was back in place.

Tasha slowed her breathing and tempered any excitement. Time to play their game. "Gladly. Just let me get my agent on the phone."

Show time.

CHAPTER NINE

"Did you read this?" Clay's bulk filled Tasha's doorway as he didn't bother to say hello.

"Read what?" she asked when she could wrest her attention from the beefy arm holding the paper and to what he'd said.

"This, this . . . piece of crap," he spat, waving the pages in the air.

Still holding the door open as he stood outside, she asked, "You mean your contract with the production company?"

"Yes." He stalked into the room and slapped the papers onto her table before spinning to face her.

"Sure, come on in." Brows raised, she closed the door since it seemed, invited or not, he was staying. She walked, a lot more calmly than he had, to where he stood. "What's the problem?"

She'd gotten the final copy of her own contract, negotiated by her agent, and had happily signed it. It wasn't quite as good of a deal as she'd had with *Good Day, San Diego*, but it was still pretty good.

Given the circumstances, she was happy. Clay,

apparently, was not. Maybe he should get himself an agent to negotiate his terms.

Clay and an agent. She smothered a chuckle at the incongruity of that idea. Though it was no more ridiculous than his being her co-host.

Meanwhile, he had yet to answer her question as, red faced, he snorted like a bull.

She picked up the papers and scanned them. It looked like the typical contract. Not a whole lot different than hers, except his contained the stuff about the property as well as his compensation. She scowled when she saw how much he'd be earning even though he had no experience at all in front of the camera.

"It looks pretty boilerplate to me. What's the problem?" she asked, looking up to see him staring at her, wide-eyed.

He sputtered. "What do you mean, what's the problem? Look at these requirements. Cameras following me around twenty-four hours a day including inside every room in my house."

Tasha held up a finger to interrupt his rant. "No, not in the bathroom."

"Yeah, great. Nice of them not to film me taking a shit." He screwed up his mouth.

She sighed at his crudeness. "It's a television show. Cameras are not negotiable. Anything else?"

"Yes, there is. She said I'd make the final decisions, but I don't see that written here anywhere. So, what? Will *you* get a say in my design?"

Insulted, she frowned. "I have excellent taste."

"I don't give a shit. It's not *my* taste and this is *my* house. You're probably going to want to strip it of everything that makes it unique and turn it into some generic soulless piece of shit." His gaze swept the surroundings, inferring her home was exactly that.

"I'm not going to try to destroy the character of the house. That's what I love about it. I'd probably switch up the exterior color though. The more I think about it, that turquoise looks a little too much like a swimming pool. But I think a nice soft pink would fit the period of the house and keep its unique character. I picked up a book of historically appropriate paint colors at the hardware store. There was one called Shrimp Pink that was beautiful."

She was about to get the booklet to show him when she noticed his expression.

"Shrimp Pink? What the fuck? No!" His eyes bulged as he shook his head. "I like the blue. It's staying."

She let out a huff. "Of course, you like it."

The color was brash and over-the-top in-your-face, just like he was.

"This isn't going to work." He shook his head and reached for the papers.

Fearing he'd tear them up and walk away from this deal, she leapt forward. "All right. The color stays. It's your choice."

He narrowed his eyes to glare at her. "I'm not sure I trust you."

"You're going to have to if you want this house." And Tasha was going to have to learn to compromise because she wasn't convinced Joanne would keep her on as the host if Clay walked away from the deal.

Somehow they'd become a package deal.

Stupid vodka. She'd never drink it again since apparently she made horrible choices while under the influence. Now she was stuck with that bad decision, twenty-four/seven for the entire shoot.

She crossed her arms and let out a huff. "I don't know what you're complaining about. I'm the one who should be upset. I have to live there with you for the duration of the show."

"Oh, yeah. Because it will be such a hardship for you to live on the beach." He rolled his eyes.

"It will be a hardship as long as you're there. It's not going to be comfortable. That house is smaller than this place and I live here alone. Living with you in that tiny bungalow is going to be a little too close for comfort."

His face twisted into an ugly hateful expression. "Don't worry, sweetheart. You don't have to be concerned about the close quarters. There's no chance of me touching you ever again. I assure you."

She didn't know whether to be relieved or insulted—and then there was that strange niggling of disappointment inside her.

Tasha planted her hand on one hip. "Fine with me. I'm certainly not looking for a repeat of the other night."

He blew out a short bark of a laugh. "Yeah, I'm sure."

She ignored the comment rather than get into a conversation that would force her to have to admit she didn't remember anything past opening the door that night, until she woke the next morning alone.

"Anyway, you have to sign the contract or you don't get your house."

"Don't remind me." He mumbled something else under his breath too.

She couldn't quite make it all out but it sounded a bit like a long list of obscenities.

"It's four weeks total, including all the post production stuff. Surely even you can survive something for that long," she said.

He sent her another glare. "As I've pointed out before, you know nothing about me, but yeah, I can and have survived worse."

Looking around him, he stalked to her kitchen counter and grabbed the pen lying next to a pad of paper. He strode back and spun the contract to face him.

Bent over the low table he flipped to the last page and scratched a large scrawl of black ink on the signature line, sealing their fate for the duration of this production.

"There." He shoved the papers forward. "You can get that back to them. I don't scan or fax or whatever the hell else they suggested I do with it. And I sure as fuck am not paying to deliver it to them by messenger.

She reached out and took the precious paperwork that would ensure her future career prospects and clutched it tight against her chest. "I'll get it to them."

Scowling, he tossed the pen down and turned toward the door, only to spin back before he took a single step. "I don't care what that paper says or doesn't say, I want it understood that I choose what happens to my house."

Tasha tipped her head. "Fine."

He stared at her for a few seconds, as if evaluating whether he could trust her or not.

Finally, he turned and yanked open the door. When it slammed shut behind him and his overwhelming presence was gone, Tasha dropped onto the sofa and sagged against the back cushions, his contract still clenched in her hand.

She glanced down at his signature, as bold and unruly as the man himself.

God, he was just so . . . so . . . she was having trouble coming up with enough descriptive words for what that man was. Obnoxious and annoying didn't seem strong enough.

She'd need a thesaurus to fully express how he made her feel. And *ugh*, she was going to have to be his roommate for a month.

So why did thinking about him make her want to break out her battery-operated boyfriend? She wished she knew.

CHAPTER TEN

"What the fuck are you doing?" Clay came to a stop outside the door of the bedroom he'd chosen as his.

The guy from the production company twisted atop the six-foot ladder to glance down and answer him. "Installing the camera."

"In my fucking bedroom?"

"Yes. They said every room except the bathroom gets one."

"Fuck." He'd known that. He'd discussed that there would be cameras in every room except in the bathroom with Tasha before he signed the damn contract almost a month ago.

So why hadn't he grasped the full ramifications of there being one in his bedroom?

Because this was all new to him. And all these Hollywood types were wheeler dealers who threw a seventeen-page contract at him knowing he wouldn't be able to understand half of it.

He'd been trying to save money and didn't want to hire a lawyer. Tasha had signed hers and said it was all standard stuff so he hadn't worried too much that they were trying to screw him.

Now he realized he should have sucked it up and spent the money.

Shit. He spun and almost crashed head-on into the other camera and Greg, the man operating it.

Unable to get over the fact he'd be monitored as he slept, he turned back to glare at the workman mounting the camera on his wall. "Why the fuck would they want hours and hours of me sleeping?"

The man turned his head to shoot Clay a look. "Sleeping? Yeah, *that's* what they want to catch on camera in your bedroom. You sleeping." He let out a snort and turned his attention back to the device as realization hit Clay.

He let out a laugh. "They think she and I are going to have sex in here?"

Jesus, these producers really were stupid, because that wasn't going to happen, and it sure as fuck wasn't going to happen while cameras filmed it.

Were they nuts? He wasn't a porn star. Not to mention his parents—shit, his grandmother too— were all going to be watching this, along with his teammates and the rest of the country.

Fucking lunacy.

As he stalked out of the room, he realized since the closing on the property that morning, and the subsequent move-in of the crew an hour later, he'd said and thought some variation of the word *fuck* a good thousand times.

Good. He hoped he cussed so much they had to bleep every other word. Maybe then they'd give him some damn privacy.

But more likely, with his crap luck, they'd sue him.

Breech of contract for reasons of obscenities.

Clay shook his head and strode down the hall, only to be stopped dead in his tracks when he saw another ladder set up in his guest room. Or, for the next month, Tasha's bedroom.

He dared to look up and yeah, there was another guy installing another camera aimed at her bed.

"Fuck." He turned and—again—narrowly missed the ever present cameraman who was practically up his ass. "Five feet, dude. Can you at least give me that? Just five fucking feet? Please!"

Greg pressed his lips tight and nodded.

No fun yelling at someone who wasn't allowed to fight back.

Clay continued in his path to the living room, but what he found there wasn't much better. Tasha, sitting in a director's type chair, getting her hair and makeup done.

"What the fuck is this?" he asked.

"Problem?" She glanced at him past the make-up chick.

"What are you doing putting on make-up and wearing that—*dress*." He did his best to not notice how hot she looked in it.

The dress was cut low in the front and slit high up the side. The whole thing was ridiculous. Who remodeled a house while wearing a formal gown and heels?

He knew this show was going to be a bunch of bullshit, but this was pushing even the low bar he'd set.

"It's just to shoot the opening sequence. I'll change later."

"Into what? Semi-formal attire instead of formal

wear? Do you even own a T-shirt?" he asked.

She opened her mouth to answer.

"And not a designer one that cost a fortune and you're afraid to get dirty," he cut her off with that condition.

When she closed her mouth again, he knew he'd been right. She owned no work clothes and the chances of her doing anything around the house except annoy him were slim to none.

He'd rather do it all alone anyway, but as per the contract she was going to have to be there for this stupid show. No doubt she was going to be in his way the entire time, flouncing around in fancy dresses and complaining about getting dirty.

"You're going to have to shoot your part for the opening sequence too, you know. You might want to do that before you get all dirty."

He shook his head. "Nope. They can edit something together from all the hours of shit they'll have. And speaking of getting dirty . . .You better go to Wal-Mart or something and get yourself some cheap Fruit of the Loom T-shirts because I'm not doing all the work by myself just because you're afraid to mess up your fancy Rodeo Drive clothes. I'm going to start scraping the popcorn off the ceiling today."

The director rushing toward him had Clay turning to see what fresh hell she brought.

"Clay."

"Yes, Maria." He somehow mustered patience he didn't know he had and answered her civilly.

"You have to avoid saying any name brands on camera."

"What?" What the fuck was she talking about?

"Wal-Mart. Fruit of the Loom. They're not our sponsors so you can't mention them on the show or our paying sponsors will get angry you're plugging the other companies for free on *Hot House*."

So now he had to walk on eggshells and watch what he said? How many times a day would he normally have drank a Mountain Dew or eaten a Subway sandwich, or said he needed to run to Home Depot for something?

A fuck ton, that's how many.

The other part of what she'd said struck him. Clay frowned. "Wait. Hot House?"

She nodded. "That's the name of the show."

In his contract they'd referred to this debacle as a cable network home renovation show, title to be determined.

Hot House. *Stupid House,* more like. But the name of the show wasn't his decision so he moved back to the more pertinent issue—their trying to muzzle what he said on camera.

"Who are our sponsors? Who *am* I allowed to mention?" he asked.

Clay supposed his luck wasn't good enough to have Budweiser as a sponsor so he could drink a nice cold beer in front of the cameras while he worked. Or even better, have Anheuser-Busch deliver a truckload of free beer to the set.

"Um, they're mostly, female products."

"Aw, jeez." He was going to be on a show sponsored by a douche company or some feminine itch product. Lovely.

"There is one sponsor you might be happy with," she continued.

"And who's that?" He could only imagine.

It had better not be some erectile dysfunction medication. As it was the guys were never going to let him live down that he had agreed to be on this damn show to begin with.

"Iron Man XXL Condoms," Maria said.

He considered that for a moment. Yeah. He could be on board with that particular sponsorship.

"All right." He nodded. "Have them send over a couple of boxes."

Her brows rose high as she looked a little too pleased about his comment. "All right. I'll get some here right away."

Clay realized his mistake immediately. The condoms. The bedroom cameras. Maria's excitement he'd asked for free condom samples . .

They truly were hoping he and Tasha were going to get busy. On camera. To be aired countrywide to anyone with cable.

Fucking unbelievable, delusional, sick motherfuckers.

He shook his head and stomped out of the room. He'd sold his soul and his dignity to these Hollywood devils for this house. But what was done, was done.

All he could do now was get to work on making it perfect—and ignore the cameras while doing it.

As the cameraman scrambled to get out of his way while he strode down the hall, Clay realized that was going to be easier said than done.

A horrible idea struck him and he stopped and turned to the cameraman, who narrowly avoided plowing into him. "Are you going to be living here too?" he asked.

Greg pressed his lips tight again, unwilling to speak. Clay stood his ground willing to wait him out until finally the cameraman said, "No. The crew goes home at night and only the installed cameras are on."

Thank God for that. At least this guy wouldn't be hovering over his bed as he slept. Only the night vision camera would be doing that.

Jesus—what the fuck had he gotten himself into?

CHAPTER ELEVEN

Hot House Renovation Day 1
I hate him! It's like living with a caveman!! A stupid,
mean one.

Pen poised in her hand, Tasha pressed her lips together and considered what else to add to her show diary.

What she'd written probably wasn't what Maria had in mind when she suggested Tasha keep a journal during the production.

They'd want fun anecdotes about what she was feeling and thinking during the shoot. Entertaining things they could talk about on interviews while promoting.

Crap. Interviews. She'd forgotten that part.

Her internment in this hell wouldn't end with the shooting of the final episode. They'd have to promote too. Talk show appearances. Interviews. Promo spots.

If *Hot House* hit big, promoting the show could involve travel and national appearances all over the damn country. She could be joined at the hip to Clay for another month or more.

She drew in a breath. If today had been any indication, they'd be scratching each other's eyes out by then.

The orders he'd barked at her during the few hours of work he'd actually done on the house was enough to make her want to pick up a hammer, all right. But not to use on a nail.

A shovel might be even better. Right up side the head—

Jeez. She never realized she had such a violent side. Apparently it took Clay and his nastiness to bring it out.

Stay out of my way.

Go sit down before you ruin it.

Then the most hurtful—the two words he'd mumbled beneath his breath—*fucking useless.*

That one was just plain mean.

Hot angry tears pricked at the back of her eyes at the memory. Joanne and Maria had said they liked the banter between them at the bar. To Tasha it had felt more like bickering than bantering, but the decision was theirs to make.

But now he was just being cruel.

Stupid, obnoxious—*grrr!* He made her so mad.

Tossing down the pen, she stood. She didn't need to write down her thoughts or feelings from today. She'd never forget them.

She stalked to one of her two suitcases.

Living in a construction zone was going to be challenging enough. Living in this tiny bedroom out of a suitcase on the floor and sleeping on a rollaway bed because there was no furniture in this damn house was going to make it even worse.

But having to be here, in a one thousand square

foot bungalow with a man who's overinflated ego and bad attitude could fill a mansion—that was going to take every fiber of strength she had in her.

Pawing through the clothes she'd brought, she searched for her toiletry bag so she could brush her teeth before he hogged the one bathroom they'd have to share.

There was no cable or even a television in the house. She might as well try to get some sleep.

Meanwhile, she owned a beautiful condo with the full HD cable package including premium channels and a large screen TV. That would sit empty while she had to rough it here with the Neanderthal.

Why couldn't she just drive home each night and back in the morning? She'd suggested it, more than once, and had been shot down in no uncertain terms.

Stupid producers.

As she pawed through the clothes with more vigor, her hand struck something long and hard and she froze.

Tasha had forgotten she'd packed *that*.

Somehow when she'd been flinging things into her suitcases she'd had the foresight that at some point during the four-week production she might need to relieve some stress . . . of the sexual nature. She certainly was stressed now, thanks to him.

A nice orgasm might help calm her down so she'd actually be able to sleep.

She glanced up at the camera mounted in the corner. She definitely couldn't do it here. Not with that camera running twenty-four/seven. The bathroom was a safe zone, however.

Glancing again at the camera, she moved in front of the suitcase, blocking the view with her body as she tried to shove the vibrator into her already overstuffed toiletry case.

It didn't fit.

Fine. On to plan B. She found her pajamas, rolled the vibrator in them, grabbed her toiletry case and carried the whole bundle across the room to the door.

It would look perfectly normal that she'd change for bed in the bathroom, given the camera situation.

In hindsight, she probably should have fought to make the bedrooms a no camera zone too. But she'd been too busy acting like the experienced professional and making Clay feel like an idiot for expecting there not to be cameras everywhere.

She hated that he'd been right to be angry. The bedroom cam was intrusive and, at the moment, damned inconvenient.

Four weeks. She repeated the mantra to herself for what had to be the dozenth time today. She only had to get through four more weeks.

CHAPTER TWELVE

He'd been hoping for a nice long shower, because lord knew he needed one. From scraping the ceiling, he had shit in his hair that might take three washings to get out. He felt dirty and gritty and covered in dust everywhere, including his damn teeth.

But, nope . . . no shower for him because just as he was grabbing his bar of soap and his towel, about to head into the bathroom, he'd heard the door snap shut.

That had been over ten minutes ago.

What the hell was she doing in there? It wasn't like she'd done any work today to get dirty. What kind of nighttime beauty ritual did she go through?

Diva—

A buzzing sound had his head whipping up. "What the hell?"

Shit. The last thing he needed was for something to be wrong with the electrical. Though if there were something wrong, best to find out now rather than later.

The wiring was old. Who knew what kind of shit

was happening in the walls where he couldn't see, something that could possibly burn down the house.

An electrical fire—Clay didn't even want to consider the possibility.

Swinging his legs over the side of the bed, he stood and padded barefoot across the cool wood floors and toward the hallway shared by the two bedrooms.

Clay glanced at Tasha's closed bedroom door. He wondered if she'd booby-trapped the entrance to keep him out while she was in the bathroom.

The way she looked at him, he wasn't sure if she hated him, feared him, or both.

Didn't she know he could get in any place at any time if he really wanted to? He not only could, but had, during his years on the team.

Quick and quiet, or with a big boom, depending on the situation, they'd breeched more doors in more countries than he could count.

No, she probably didn't know that since he'd never told her what he'd done while in the Navy and he didn't plan on it.

It wouldn't be hard to avoid the topic. She obviously wasn't at all interested in actually talking to him about anything more than her bitching over the construction.

Though keeping his past from the producers once they really started to promote this stupid show might be more difficult.

It didn't matter if they did find out he'd been on SEAL Team One. He was retired now. But it was the principal.

After two decades of serving his country, he deserved his privacy now. But Clay had a feeling he'd sacrificed all rights to a private life when he'd signed that contract.

It was a problem he'd deal with if and when it arose. Right now, he had to figure out why the buzzing coming from the bathroom had kicked up a notch, getting louder and faster.

The bathroom door was closed and as far as he knew Tasha was still inside, taking her sweet time, torturing him so he couldn't shower off the day's construction dust and dirt.

He crept closer and the buzzing had definitely grown louder and was no doubt coming from the bathroom.

Was it a problem with the water heater and not the electric? That was less frightening but still horrifying. Clay could do carpentry and other small repairs but he knew shit about plumbing.

What he did know was that plumbers cost an arm and a leg, when you could get them to come at all.

But he didn't hear the water running. Not in the shower or the sink.

Was she shaving her legs with an electric razor maybe? Did women even do that?

Women were the last great mystery all his years in the SEALs hadn't solved. Did lady razors have two settings—a low and then a high for extra difficult hair?

Exactly where was that extra thick hair on Tasha and why was she shaving it? The possibilities were as intriguing as they were horrifying.

Another sound joined the electronic buzz, but this one was decidedly human.

He might not know shit about lady razors, but he knew an orgasm when he heard one. And that meant the source of the formerly unidentified buzz was no longer in doubt.

Clay closed his mouth after he noticed it had dropped open.

The mystery noise wasn't the water heater or the wires. It wasn't a razor either.

Nope. There was no question in his mind—Tasha was getting herself off with a vibrator and *holy shit* the image of her in there doing that just feet from where he stood had him instantly hard.

He might not like the woman all that much, but apparently his body liked the idea of what she was doing.

Reaching down, he tried to adjust his length as it pressed painfully against the seam in his shorts.

Yup. His planned shower just got a little longer because besides the dust in his hair, he now had to also deal with the growing problem in his shorts.

Damn woman, torturing him even when he wasn't in the same room with her. That figured. He'd come to expect nothing less from her.

The only question was how he was going to deal with this for four more weeks.

CHAPTER THIRTEEN

She'd actually slept. A deep, dreamless, rejuvenating sleep that had her waking refreshed when the sunlight streamed relentlessly through the mini-blinds on the curtain-less windows and hit her in the face. But she hadn't even minded that. She'd sprung up, showered, dressed and made coffee all before most people were out of bed for the day.

It was amazing. A miracle actually. Definitely not what she had expected when she'd preemptively put a bottle of water and a bottle of sleeping pills on the floor next to her bed last night, just in case.

It also made no sense. The bed was foreign to her and not exactly comfortable. Her bedroom was on the wrong side of the house to hear the ocean—thanks to Clay choosing the good bedroom that faced the water for himself—and she'd forgotten to pack her sound machine.

Even so, she'd been out like a light for a solid eight hours.

Her gaze hit upon her suitcase. She'd buried B.O.B., her battery-operated boyfriend, deep beneath her clothes last night after a nice long session with him in the bathroom.

Could that be the reason for her great night's sleep?

If it was, she was going to do it every night because it was better than any pill or sound machine. But she was going to have to get new batteries because he definitely was not performing up to capacity, one reason it had taken so long for her to finish.

Clay might have some. She remembered seeing him loading up a flashlight yesterday with fresh batteries. He was in the bathroom now. She'd heard him go in a few minutes ago.

The crew hadn't arrived yet for the day. This was the perfect time to search.

Creeping through the doorway, she glanced left and then right. The hall was clear.

Like a ninja, she kicked off her sandals that would make far too much noise on the wood floor and ran barefoot to the living room.

His toolbox was in the corner of the room, right where she'd seen it yesterday. With any luck she'd find what she needed inside.

She bent over the metal box, refusing to kneel down on the dust covered floor since Clay hadn't swept up very well when he'd finished yesterday.

There was a lot of stuff inside. Big heavy metal stuff that sounded like a freight train when she tried to move it to the side to see what was beneath.

His tools weren't very organized. If she piled all of

her makeup into one big box with no organization like this, she'd never find a thing.

"What the devil are you pawing around in there for?"

Guilty, she squeaked with surprise. She yanked her hands out of the box, straightened and spun to face him.

The bastard had snuck up on her. Again. For a big guy, he sure moved quietly. Must be those ratty old sneakers he insisted on wearing around the house.

"Uh. Nothing. I, uh, I just needed some batteries."

"Oh, really?" Folding his arms over his broad chest, he smirked. "And what kind of batteries did you need?"

"Double A."

Watching her too closely, he moved to a drawer in the kitchen. "I put some in here yesterday. Two enough?" he asked.

Her cheeks heated. "Um, actually four."

"Four?" His brows shot high. "Must be a powerful little device. What did you say these were for?" he asked, holding the package of batteries hostage in his big hand.

"Um, a clock radio." It was the only thing she could think of and it was ridiculous. She didn't even own a clock radio, never mind one that ran on batteries. She used her cell phone as an alarm and to listen to music.

Maybe the Neanderthal was old school and wouldn't question her.

"A battery-operated clock radio?" His lips twitched. "Is the electrical outlet in your bedroom not working? I'd better check it." He started toward the hall leading toward the bedrooms.

She scurried to beat him to her door, not sure she'd hidden her battery-operated friend well enough under the clothes in her suitcase, which was on the floor right below the outlet.

"No! It works," she said much too loudly. When he paused and that dark brow quirked up again, she scrambled to explain. "The outlet works, but I like to carry the clock radio around and, uh, take it places with me. You know, to use as a radio. So that's why I need batteries."

"Places like the bathroom, you mean?" he asked with more amusement than the question warranted.

"Um, yeah. Sometimes."

"Okay. Here you go." Still smirking, he finally handed her the batteries.

"Thank you. I appreciate it."

"I bet you do." With a snort, he headed out of the room, shaking his head as he left.

That man was a strange one. Too bad his odd behavior did nothing to diminish his hotness. She wished it did. Wished that she could be completely repulsed by him instead of turned on. Then she wouldn't have needed his stupid batteries or her battery-operated boyfriend in the first place.

"So, when you're done with your batteries for your, uh, radio, you want to come with me to Home Dep—um, the store?" he asked.

"Me?" Her eyes widened. Was he actually inviting her somewhere willingly?

"Yes, you." He laughed.

"Why?"

"Why?" He frowned. "Because I'm going to pick

out the new tile for the bathroom and I thought you might want to be there. You know, since you spend so much time in there."

His continued references to the bathroom had her eyes narrowing but she decided not to argue with his exaggeration and tell him that she did not spend a lot of time in the bathroom.

She'd enact her revenge on him later, at the store when she fought for her choice of tile.

There was no doubt in her mind that Clay was a four-inch square, plain white tile kind of guy, while she was more of a blue glass subway tile kind of girl.

The only question in her mind was why he was really inviting her, because he sure didn't want or value her opinion. It was probably so he could make fun of her for being out of her element in the store.

She'd show him. Clay might not really want her opinion but he was going to get it. Since Maria liked when she and Clay disagreed she should really love this.

"I'd love to come. Thank you."

If he was surprised by her answer, he didn't show it. He nodded and turned toward the other room, before glancing back over his shoulder. "Can you be ready to go in half an hour? Or do you need more bathroom time?"

She scowled at his smug expression and his question.

What the hell did he think she needed all that time for? She was already dressed and ready for the day. He was just making fun of her, as usual.

Not dignifying his veiled insult by arguing, she said, "Half an hour is fine."

Tasha followed that up with the sweetest smile she could muster, then turned on her heel and headed for her room, batteries in hand.

In her suitcase, besides her hidden vibrator, she had the notebook with style ideas she'd collected. And while Clay had been grunting and cursing at the ceiling he was scraping yesterday, she'd walked around and taken measurements of all the rooms in the house, including the bathroom. She'd bet he hadn't done that.

Ha! She'd prove to Clay she wasn't *fucking useless* like he thought she was, maybe even make him apologize for that comment, and it would be a sweet day when he did.

CHAPTER FOURTEEN

Clay sighed. "What is your problem? You're looking at me like I'm speaking Mandarin."

Asher shook his head and said, "You might as well be since I really don't understand a word you're saying."

"What exactly don't you understand?"

"All of it."

"It's not that difficult. They let me buy the house if I let them record the renovations and have the TV chick stay in the house for the duration of the show."

"And you had to sneak out to meet me tonight because otherwise they would have sent a cameraman to follow you."

"Yup." Clay nodded but that last part hadn't been as simple as Asher had made it sound.

When Clay had made the mistake of mentioning he was going out tonight, Maria had jumped at the chance to be able to get his guys' night on tape. He'd been forced to lie and say his plans had changed, that his friend had had to cancel, and then use all his skills to slip out of the house undetected.

He'd gone out the damn bathroom window so the cameras mounted throughout the house wouldn't see him leaving. But the extra effort had been necessary because as bad as Clay having to be on camera was, it would be far worse for Asher, still an active duty SEAL stationed at Coronado.

Clay couldn't have Greg follow him to a well-known SEAL bar to meet his SEAL friend. There'd be no hiding what he was after that and he'd be damned if the producers profited off his service by using the fact he was a frogman to promote their stupid show.

"Yeah, see that right there. All of what you just said. It doesn't make any sense. You hate reality shows. You're allergic to cameras. And you hate those Hollywood-type TV stars—" Asher's eyes widened. "Oh. Wait. She's hot, isn't she?"

"What?" Clay frowned. "No. That's not it."

"She's not hot?" Asher lifted a brow. "So they hired her to star in their TV show because she's hideous?"

"No." Clay drew his brows lower and glared at his teammate. "Shut up. That's not what I'm saying. Yeah, she's pretty in a TV kind of way but that's not why I'm doing this."

"Mmm, hmm." Asher smiled as he nodded.

"Fuck you." Clay didn't need this sarcasm from his supposed friend. "I'm doing this because if I didn't, I was going to lose the property. They had God knows how big of a budget they could have used to bid the price up."

"The location does look pretty sweet in the pictures."

"It is. And I wasn't going to lose it to some

Hollywood production company who only wanted it for a month."

"Still doesn't hurt the deal comes with some live-in booty though." Asher grinned.

Clay rolled his eyes. "Shut up. There's no booty."

His cell phone in his hand, Asher shook his head. "Nope. I'm not buying it. If you haven't already tapped that, or at least tried to, you want to. Because, I mean look at her."

Asher held up his phone to face Clay and a picture of Tasha filled his screen.

"How the fuck . . ."

"I looked her up." Asher grinned with satisfaction.

"How?"

"You said she was a minor local celebrity named Tasha. I searched online and she came right up. Did you know she used to host *Good Day, San Diego*?"

"No." He honestly hadn't known because unlike his friend, Clay had never bothered to search Tasha online.

He knew enough about the woman from real life. He didn't need the web to tell him about the fake stuff she put out there for the public.

"You know the day her show got cancelled she had a meltdown on air that went viral?" Asher asked.

No, he hadn't known. Clay paused with his martini halfway to his mouth. "Really?"

"Oh yeah. It's all over YouTube. Somebody even set it to music. It's pretty funny."

All right, now *that* he had to see. "Cue that shit up for me." Clay smiled.

"Thought you might be interested in that." He handed his cell to Clay and continued, "She's still hot though."

Hot enough to have Clay jerking off in the shower when he finally got into the bathroom last night. Hot enough to keep him tossing and turning for half the night to fantasies of her and the vibrator. But he'd endure torture before admitting that to his buddy.

"No comment," he said, and hit play on the video and there she was.

And holy shit, she was wearing the outfit he'd met her in. He frowned and glanced at the date on the video.

The timing was about right. He'd met her the day she'd been fired and had a meltdown on air.

It had to be the same day. That was why she'd been so drunk in the middle of the day. He remembered well exactly how drunk. Drunk enough to pass out on him before he got to finish the job she'd invited him in to perform.

When the first video led to another one of her, this time not set to music, he leaned in close to listen to what she was saying. He could see the tears of hurt and anger shining in her eyes as she spoke.

Damn, this explained a lot.

When the video ended, he hit to replay it. Listening closer this time from the start.

He'd never been fired, but he'd been passed over for promotion once during his career and it had sucked.

It had made him work doubly hard to make sure he'd never be passed over again.

Was this home renovation show Tasha's version of doubling down to make sure she didn't get fired again? Was that why she had fought him at every turn today on camera while they were in the tile section of Home Depot?

He was having trouble mustering his usual level of annoyance toward her after seeing the video. That pissed him off. He didn't want to like her.

Clay let out a huff and tossed Asher's cell onto the table between them, pissed off at him too for mentioning the stupid video in the first place.

Nothing had changed. He was going to get through this four weeks and that was that.

She could save her career on her own time, when it didn't involve him or his house.

CHAPTER FIFTEEN

Clay might have snuck out of the house, but he'd be damned if he snuck back in. He swung open the front door and found Tasha sitting in one of the chairs set around the folding table in the living room.

She'd jumped in her seat when he opened the door.

Frowning, she asked, "I didn't see you go out. When did you leave?"

"Before." His focus moved to her laptop screen where he saw a disturbing image—a picture of himself. "What's that? What are you watching?"

"The footage of us at the store."

He rolled his eyes. "Great."

"Apparently it is great. Maria emailed this clip to me and told me to watch it because she wants more just like it." She scowled, looking as unhappy as Clay felt.

Good. At least he wasn't alone in his misery.

Drawing in a breath he moved closer. She angled the screen so he could see from where he stood behind her, and then she pushed the button to raise the volume.

He watched himself on the screen as he shook his head and said, "No."

"Why not?" she asked on the video. "It's the hot new thing."

"Which means it's a fad," he said.

"No. It means it will give the house a fresh new, up-to-date modern look."

On screen, he audibly snorted. "Yeah, tell all the people who are stuck with bad choices from a few decades ago that."

"It's not like I'm telling you to buy those new black kitchen appliances that I've seen around."

"Good, because I'm not going to and it's my house."

"That deed you keep flinging in my face obviously didn't come with any taste."

"Oh, nice." He nodded. "Watch out, sweetheart, the real you is showing."

She sighed. "I'm just saying that this tile is fresh but classic."

He blew out a huff. "White is classic."

"White is boring," she countered. "And you are stubborn and set in your ways."

"My way works just fine for me." On screen, Clay set his legs wide and folded his arms.

He glanced down at himself now.

Standing in the living room while frowning at what he saw on the video, he realized he was in the exact same pose as the version of him on the screen.

He uncrossed his arms but then didn't know what to do with them as they hung at his sides. Fuck it. He crossed them over his chest again and gave up. No changing who he was now.

The camera moved to focus on the expression of the store employee unfortunate enough to get caught in their argument.

"Can't we just buy a few of each and bring them home? Lay them out and see?" Tasha asked.

"No." He shook his head. "I'm not going to be stuck with tile I don't like and can't return when I don't use it."

The kid in the orange vest raised his hand before he said, "Actually, you can return the unused tiles. No problem. Just save your receipt."

Clay shot the boy a glare then looked back to Tasha. "Fine. Buy the damn tile."

She smiled in victory as the camera caught his displeasure. That's when the clip ended.

Tasha leaned back from the computer. "That's what Maria wants more of."

He let out a laugh. "Well the good news is she's probably going to get it."

To his surprise, Tasha let out a short laugh of her own. "I hate to agree with you, but I think you're right."

"See. We can agree," he said.

She laughed again and looked up at him. Her face was scrubbed clean of makeup and her hair was in a ponytail.

Her pink tank top was tight and there was definitely no bra beneath it. Her pink and white polka-dotted pajama pants were about a size too big and tied at the waist. Her bare feet stuck out from the bottom as she sat cross-legged in the chair.

It was the complete opposite of how he was used to seeing her. The change threw him.

He realized she'd said something that he'd

completely missed. "Um, what?"

"I said, I laid out the tiles in the bathroom to see how they look."

The bathroom. The one room he probably shouldn't go into with her looking so tempting. Especially not after he'd seen that clip from *Good Day, San Diego* that had made her seem more like a human rather than the evil witch from hell he'd seen her as since day one.

And he especially shouldn't follow her into the bathroom after what he'd heard her doing in there last night.

"You wanna see?" she asked, sounding soft and sweet and damn, her nipples were hard. Shit.

He yanked his gaze up from her chest and cleared his throat. "Ugh, all right."

Shit. He'd planned on saying no. That they could look in the morning when the crew was there. Now they were going to be in the bathroom alone with no camera watching them.

He followed her as she led the way and his head spun.

Even if he was weak at the moment thanks to her obscenely tight and tiny top, he had nothing to worry about because she disliked him as much as he disliked her.

There was no way they'd accidentally have sex, because she'd never let him touch her again.

Good. Phew. Crisis averted.

He walked in behind her as she flipped on the light and turned, glancing up at him.

Her top teeth latched onto her bottom lip and it was all he could focus on as he imagined biting that lip for himself. Right before he envisioned her mouth closing over his cock.

Fuck.

"Well?" she asked.

"Well, what?"

"What do you think of the glass tile?" she asked.

He forced his gaze to where she'd leaned a row of tile against the wall on the edge of the tub and—*double fuck*—he liked it.

Her stupid blue tile looked really good. Clean. Nautical. Even masculine.

"Shit." He ran his hand over his chin and let out a breath.

"You don't like it." Her mood visibly deflated as her head tipped down and her shoulders slumped.

"No. I do like it."

Her head whipped up and her eyes brightened. "You do?"

"Yes. And if you say I told you so, I'll buy the other tile just to spite you."

She pressed her lips tight together and shook her head. "I won't say it. I promise."

A small smile began to bow her lips and he shook his head. She might not say it, but no doubt she was thinking it and enjoying this moment way too much.

There was nothing he could do but let her—and get out of this damn room before the image of her in those damn tempting PJs haunted him all damn night.

"Good night, Tasha." He turned for the door.

"Night, Clay."

Stupid Asher. This was his fault for putting the idea of them being together in his head. He had to blame somebody and he'd be damned if that somebody was himself.

He shook his head all the way to his room and then slammed the door. It was going to be a long night.

CHAPTER SIXTEEN

Stupid man.

Now he liked the tile she chose? The same tile he'd fought against tooth and nail at the store. What the hell was that about?

It must be some sort of trick. She'd noticed he didn't say he liked it on camera.

Oh no. Instead it had been mumbled in the bathroom where there were no cameras and when the crew wasn't around to witness it.

That figured. Tomorrow he'd probably change his mind. Do a one-eighty on camera to make her look like a crazy person.

Tasha stomped out of the bathroom and into her bedroom down the hall. Her suitcase caught her eye and she paused, remembering the fresh batteries she'd installed in the device hidden inside.

She could go to bed, but she was so angry, chances were she wouldn't be able to sleep. Or she could grab her battery-operated boyfriend, head back to the bathroom, relieve some stress, and then have a restful sleep like she had last night.

Ignoring the fact that it seemed the angrier Clay made her, the more awake her lady-parts got, she walked to the suitcase.

Blocking the camera's view with her body she shoved B.O.B. under her shirt, grabbed her toiletry case as cover, and strode to the bathroom before Clay got in there before her.

She should have taken care of this before, when he'd been mysteriously absent.

There were two issues with that regret. One she hadn't known he'd left the house—and still couldn't figure out how he'd gotten out without her noticing. Two, she hadn't been angry and horny then.

She needed a word to describe this new phenomenon. Hangry was used to describe someone who was hungry and angry. What could she call being horny and angry instead?

Horngry, perhaps? That might work—not that she'd ever admit to having these feelings the constant arguing with Clay roused inside her.

Coming up with her new word had amused her right out of her bad mood, but that didn't mean she wasn't still primed and ready for a little toy-assisted release.

Thank God the bathroom was a camera-free zone. That thought had crossed her mind more often than she'd ever imagined it would as she peeled off her pajama bottoms and settled herself on the edge of the tub.

She'd barely turned on the device, and definitely hadn't had enough time to really start to enjoy it, before pounding on the bathroom door had her jumping.

She dropped the vibrator and had to scramble to

retrieve it as it made an even louder racket than usual while it shimmied across the floor.

While she struggled to hit the off button, the pounding sounded again, this time accompanied by Clay's voice. "Tasha! Open the door."

What the hell was going on? Was the house on fire? Was a tsunami on the way? Those were the only two reasons she could come up with as she spun in a circle, searching for a place to hide B.O.B..

"Hold on a sec," she yelled back as she shoved the vibrator under the towel and then scooped up her pajama bottoms from the floor.

She nearly fell putting them on when her foot got caught in the fabric.

When she was finally dressed, but not happy, she unlocked the door and yanked it open.

"What's wr—" She never finished her question.

Clay, wild-eyed and panting as if he'd run a marathon, leaned with both hands braced against the doorframe.

He looked crazed. Why?

"What's wrong?" This time she got the question out, genuinely concerned for both of their safety— until she swept her gaze down his body and noticed the massive tent in his shorts.

Oh, my.

She swallowed and brought her focus back to his face. "Clay?"

"Why are you doing this when I'm right here?" His nostrils flared as he drew in quick breaths.

"What are you talking about?" she asked.

He pushed into the room, forcing her to take a step back. Clay closed the door to the hallway and when he turned back to her he was standing much closer than he had been before.

She was cornered as he leaned against the sink, bracketing her with his Popeye arms and putting his face just a breath away from hers.

"You know what I'm talking about." He twisted his head to glance around the small space, before looking back at her with a sneer. "Where'd you hide the vibrator?"

Busted.

She opened her mouth to protest but it was no use. Offense seemed like her only defense so she switched gears and said, "What I do in the privacy of the bathroom is my own business."

"It's not when I have to lay in that bed on the other side of this wall and listen to it every fucking night."

Her spatial awareness really did suck. She hadn't realized that because of a jog in the hallway that put Clay's door around the corner. And it was on a different side of the house than her room, but he was right. His bedroom would share a wall with the bathroom.

"I'm sorry."

He shook his head at her apology, looking angrier than the circumstances warranted.

Finally he said, "I'm right here."

The intensity of his words, bit out with a force only a man his size could accomplish, blew the hair that had fallen across her forehead.

He couldn't be suggesting what she thought he might be suggesting.

"But you hate me," she said, baffled and confused.

His nostrils flared again. "Hate is a strong word."

Were they really going to argue over semantics at a

time like this? When his hard-on was ready to bust through his shorts and her body was screaming for attention.

"Fine. You dislike me then," she said, breathing a bit heavier too. From his closeness. From the prospect of repeating that night between them that she couldn't remember.

God, how she wished she could remember. It had to have been good. A man with emotions this intense—even if at the moment that emotion was anger—had to be good in bed.

"No more than you dislike me," he said, his eyes never leaving hers.

They were really nice eyes too. Why hadn't she appreciated exactly how nice before? Probably because they were always slits as he scowled and glared at her.

"What are you saying, Clay?"

He dropped his gaze to her lips before bringing it back up. He leaned closer, hovering barely a breath from her lips. "I've had enough with this frigging conversation. Yes or no, Tasha? One word. That's all I want. Yes or no?"

Her pulse racing, she managed to say between breaths, "Yes."

His mouth was on hers in a second. Pressed close, he crushed her between the unyielding porcelain and his rock hard body.

He thrust one hand into her hair and yanked her head back, opening her to him. Their tongues tangled as he angled his head and kissed her hard and deep, but she was having trouble focusing on anything other than the hard length pressing against her stomach.

Clay was too tall. Their parts didn't line up properly when they were standing, which was a shame because she desperately needed that one part about six inches lower.

His fingers on the elastic waistband of her bottoms nearly had her groaning in anticipation as he yanked her pajama pants to the floor.

She kicked them off her feet, leaving her naked from the waist down and desperate for relief from this ache inside her.

With his hands on her waist, he hoisted her up, perching her on the edge of the sink. The heat of his rough palms seared her bare skin.

The size of his hands, big enough to span halfway across her back as he held her, made her feel small. Vulnerable. Taken.

She liked the feeling even if it was contrary to everything she'd believed about herself as a take-charge, independent, strong woman.

Long thick fingers pressed inside her and her mouth opened on a gasp.

Clay sucked in a breath and stepped between her legs, forcing her thighs wider as he began working her hard with his fingers.

She was so needy, so ready, she felt the orgasm building. Her muscles tightened, primed for release.

With his right hand still working her, Clay reached down with his left hand and freed his erection from his shorts. Then he was leaning toward her once again.

Tasha closed her eyes, waiting for the kiss . . . the kiss that never came.

She heard the snap of the latch on the medicine cabinet next to her head and opened her eyes to see

Clay reaching inside to get—a box of Iron Man XXL Condoms?

Her eyes flew wide. "You bought condoms?"

What the hell? He was expecting this to happen with her? Or worse, was he setting up this house—nay, this construction site—for sex with other women while she was living in it with him?

"They're sponsors. Maria put them there." His voice was rough as he spoke while stretching the latex over his length.

XXL, indeed. Wow.

She brought her gaze back up as Clay leaned forward again, only this time it was to grasp her hips as he slid inside her.

A gasp escaped her lips as her body gripped on to what she'd been sorely missing.

The sensation of being filled completely while he pressed on her clit was all she needed to send her over the edge. She cried out as the orgasm hit her hard.

He palmed the back of her head and held her face against his bare chest, all without slowing the thrust of his body into hers.

The combination of his hand and cock extended the spasms and she relished each and every incredible one, from the first tingle to the final aftershock.

She heard his grunt accompany each stroke into her until finally he held deep and let out a long low groan. She felt every pulse of his release inside her. It was a spectacular reawakening to a sex life that had been a dried up wasteland for too long.

Tonight had certainly broken that drought—although she supposed the one-night she couldn't remember had technically broken her dry spell. She wasn't going to count that since she didn't recall any of it.

Damn, had that night been as good as tonight?

That made it extra tragic she couldn't recall a thing, because only B.O.B. had ever given her a climax this long. This intense.

No human man ever had. No man except for Clay.

Why did it have to be him? The one man she couldn't get along with. The man she had a definite hate-hate relationship with. Or at least a deep mutual dislike, as they'd discussed before this surreal sexual encounter.

He was still inside her. Still panting. Still fisting her hair as he held her tight against him.

She felt the heat of his sweat-dampened skin beneath her cheek. Felt the pounding of his heart. Smelled the scent of him—a masculine mixture of good clean sweat and spicy deodorant.

The sink had to be the most uncomfortable place she'd ever had sex, but she didn't mind. He felt good inside her, even as his erection faded. It was like she'd denied herself for so long that her body was starving and greedy. Now that she'd fed it, it wasn't about to go without again.

That was going to be a problem for so many reasons, the least of which was the two-hundred pounds of bad attitude now pulling away from her while looking just as mad as he had before they'd had sex.

While shaking his head, Clay stepped back. He flushed the condom and tucked himself back into his shorts.

With one final glance at her, he yanked open the door and stalked away without even a single word.

What the hell?

More confused than ever, and not as satisfied as she should be considering the mind-blowing sex, she braced both hands on the sink and jumped down.

She closed the door that Clay had left open and turned on the shower.

When she went to move the towel, she spotted B.O.B. and seriously considered going for round two since sex with Clay was like eating Chinese food. It was great when you were in the midst of it, but too soon afterward you were ready for more.

She glanced at the wall between her and Clay and decided against going for another big O on her own.

His hearing her turn on the vibrator now might really throw him over the edge. She put it down on the sink before stepping over the edge of the tub and under the shower spray.

Good sex was sweaty business so she had some cleaning up to do. A lot of thinking to do too, because tonight had to have been the strangest interaction she'd ever had with any man, never mind one she had to work with *and* live with.

The crew would be back in about eight hours. Then what? She could only hope the cameras hadn't picked up the sounds that were no doubt coming out of the bathroom, in spite of Clay nearly smothering her to keep her quiet.

Tasha sighed.

Tomorrow was going to be an interesting day.

CHAPTER SEVENTEEN

"Clay?"

His back stiffened when he heard Tasha behind him.

The dead last thing he wanted to do was turn around and see her—and remember last night.

He'd lost his mind. Obviously. That's the only excuse he could come up with for how he'd practically broken down the bathroom door to get to her.

Christ. What a mess.

But the crew was here and the cameras were rolling and so, after yet another restless night of shitty sleep, he had to play nice.

That didn't mean he had to look at her. Head down, he made himself very busy with stirring the paint primer as he said, "Yeah?"

"Can we look at those tile samples in the bathroom now? That way we can figure out how much we need and order it to be delivered to the store."

The bathroom. The scene of the crime. Why did it

have to be the bathroom she wanted to go to?

Though maybe it would knock the memories of last night out of his head to have both of them jammed in there along with the cameraman and the light guy and any other assorted crew whose job titles he didn't know but who followed him around all day anyway.

"Sure. Let's look." He stayed facing away from her, bending to grab a tape measure out of his tool box, then stopping by their one folding table to grab the yellow pad of paper and carpenter pencil there so he could write down the measurements.

His props in hand, he headed to the bathroom and pointedly did not look at Tasha's ass in the jean shorts. He really needed to get the new A/C unit installed. Maybe if he kept the house ice cold she'd wear more damn clothing.

Why the fuck was he getting hard?

He moved the pad down a bit so it hid his crotch from view. It had been barely eight hours since he'd been with her. He should be satisfied.

Crap. Now he was really hard.

No more thinking about that or her.

"So which samples did you like best?" she asked.

He frowned while facing the wall and extending the tape measure. "I told you already."

"Tell me again," she said in a voice that held more of a lilt than it should.

He turned to stare at her and caught her smile before she hid it and it all became clear. She wanted him to admit on camera that she was right and he'd been wrong. That he did like her stupid blue glass tile even if it did cost more than the plain white one.

What a bitch move. She couldn't just accept that

she'd won this round? She had to mock him and make him admit it to a million cable viewers too?

He set his jaw and desperately wanted to change his mind and order the white tile instead. That would be petty and immature and would likely send her into a screaming tizzy . . . and he liked the idea the more he thought about it.

"The plain white tile. That's what I like. That's what we're ordering."

Her eyes popped wide, as did her mouth. "Clay!"

She literally stomped her foot as she said it, which Greg hopefully caught since he'd been focused on her at the time.

Perfect. Nothing like showing her acting like a little brat. She wanted to play this game, he'd play.

He turned toward the camera and winked right at the lens, before glancing back at Tasha, who was red faced and glaring.

"Just kidding. I like the blue. We'll go with that. And jeez, try to take a joke next time, okay? No sense of humor at all, I swear." He shook his head and turned back to the wall to take that measurement again, because he'd be damned if he could remember the number anymore.

She sputtered behind him before storming out of the bathroom. He couldn't help his smile.

Oh yeah. This was fun. Torture the co-host might be his new favorite game.

Now if he could just keep his dick in his pants, it would be all good.

Clay's theory that once he'd finally had her she'd be out of his system and he could ignore her until the end of production wasn't working out too well.

He realized that the moment the crew left for the

evening and she headed into the bathroom to shower.

His mind conjured images of the night before and added a few new ones. Tasha, naked and wet, hands pressed up against the wall as he took her from behind.

He'd been working on the assumption that she'd been driving him nuts, physically, because of that first aborted night they hadn't spent together even though she thought they had. He'd been wrong.

One taste of her didn't quench his desire. Quite the opposite.

Instead, it had left him tossing all night, deciding exactly how stupid it had been to go in that bathroom. And wondering why he wanted to do it again, soon.

Tonight wasn't looking to be any different. His single-minded focus was that damn woman.

A repeat couldn't happen.

If the cameras caught anything—him going into the bathroom after her, the sounds that were coming out of that room—the producers would no doubt latch onto it like a dog with a bone.

Between what had actually happened and what they could do with editing, it could become a full-blown sex tape.

That was the last thing he needed. He hadn't wanted to be on television in the first place. He sure as hell didn't want his sex life made public for the national viewing audience.

Nope. It had been a lapse in judgment brought on by a sleepless night and visions of her and her vibrator right on the other side of his wall.

His mind was made up. He wasn't going to succumb to weakness again . . . but if she broke out that damn vibrator tonight—

No. She wouldn't do it. Not after he'd charged in there last night. He didn't give her much credit for common sense, but she had to be smart enough to not tempt him again. If she weren't intelligent enough to figure that out, hopefully she'd at least be frightened enough of him to restrain herself.

Shit. He couldn't take the chance. It wasn't in him to put all of his faith in a woman. Especially one he didn't know all that well, and who he disagreed with at almost every turn.

His liking her stupid blue tile had been an exception, not the rule. In everything else they were polar opposites and he was fine with that. It would make it easier to make sure there was never a repeat of last night.

But just in case—Clay reached into his bag and grabbed his PT clothes. Since all else had failed to distract him from thoughts of sex with Tasha, he'd work the lust out of him.

A good long hard run on the beach should do it. By the time he got back he'd be ready to pass out, with no energy for sex or anything else.

Perfect.

CHAPTER EIGHTEEN

"So how's it going with the caveman?" Jane asked.

Tasha cradled the cell on her shoulder and tried to push the memory of last night's amazing sex out of her head.

Instead, she focused on the other sixteen or so hours of waking hell he'd put her through today.

She couldn't tell her former co-worker about the bathroom sex, so she said, "He's still living up to his Neanderthal reputation."

"Maybe, but damn, he's hot."

Tasha frowned. She hadn't sent Jane a picture of Clay. "How do you know?"

"There's press up for the show."

"What? There is?" How did she not know this? And Clay definitely didn't know it either or he would have bitched about it. "Where?"

"The show's got pages on all the major social sites. I googled and the YouTube page came up as the first listing. There's a promo video posted. It's getting good views and likes too."

"A video? Of what?"

"You two. It's kind of like a montage of clips cut together and let me tell you, you two make one hell of a hot couple."

"Don't believe everything you see. We are definitely not a couple." But at least this video was good, unlike the last one of her on-air meltdown.

That one had gone viral but the chances of this *Hot House* promo video doing the same were slim to none.

She sighed as Jane continued, "Why aren't you trying to get with that hot piece of man? You're living together, aren't you? Let me tell you, the way he looks at you . . . that right there would be enough to make my panties drop."

"You mean when he's glaring at me like he hates me? I guess it's a good thing you're not here then, because I get that look from him a lot." Even as she said it, her cheeks burned, because Jane wasn't too far off from the truth.

Tasha hadn't been wearing panties at the time, but all it had taken was the intensity of Clay's stare to have her pajama bottoms hitting the bathroom floor last night.

"So where is Mr. Hunky and Handsome now? Is he like doing shirtless push-ups on the living room floor?" Jane's voice sounded dreamy as she no doubt pictured that very thing.

Tasha scoffed at that. Somehow Clay managed to have some pretty drool-worthy muscles, yet she never saw him actually doing anything to get them. Not lifting weights. Not doing push-ups. And the man made food disappear like an industrial-sized garbage disposal.

It was just one more reason to resent him since

when she ate even a little bit too much she gained weight.

So the answer to Jane's question was a resounding no. Clay was definitely not shirtless and sweaty doing push-ups. And thank God for that because the image of him, muscles bulging as he lowered himself over her, was a little too tempting.

She let out a huff. "He's not even here. He keeps sneaking out at night even though we're not supposed to go out and do anything without a camera crew with us."

Although, his breaking the rules for the second night in a row might provide a much needed opportunity. She considered a quick session with B.O.B. before he got back from wherever he'd gone off to.

Jane sucked in a breath. "Oh my God. I bet he's got a girlfriend."

"What? Why would you say that?" Tasha asked, her heart suddenly pounding.

Not that she was jealous or wanted him for herself or anything—far from it—but he'd better not have a girlfriend if he was banging her on the bathroom sink not even an hour after he arrived home from being with this other woman.

"Why else would he sneak out?" Jane asked.

"I don't know. Lot's of reasons." If only Tasha could think of a few . . .

"Name one," Jane challenged.

Put on the spot, her mind spun as she grasped for a good reason. "Um, he could be doing something embarrassing he doesn't want on camera. Like going to the proctologist or something."

Jane laughed. "At night? Two nights in a row?"

Tasha frowned. "Okay, so that was a bad example. It could be anything. An AA meeting or, um, a church service."

The problem with that theory was she saw him drink all the time but never to excess and she'd never seen him pray, not even to say grace before eating so it was doubtful he was attending nightly prayer meetings.

Her powers of deduction really did suck.

"Or he's sneaking off to a woman's house and he doesn't want her on camera. But that's a good thing."

Tasha lifted a brow. "And why is that a good thing?"

She didn't see any bright side while her stomach twisted because the secret girlfriend theory was currently the frontrunner as the most logical explanation for his repeated nighttime absences.

"If he doesn't want the relationship public, that means it's not serious. It's casual or, even better, just a fling. A two-night stand. He probably is going to dump her and never see her again, so that's why he doesn't want her on the show." Jane sounded so excited.

Her friend and former co-worker wouldn't be so happy if she realized that the only two-night stand in Clay's life that Tasha was certain of, was herself.

Jane's prediction was probably spot-on—Clay would move on from Tasha too and never want to see her again after the show was over.

This conversation had done nothing but depress her, which was ridiculous because she did not want anything more—or anything at all—with Clay.

So why was she feeling so depressed?

As much as she loved Jane, it was time to wrap up

this call. "Hey, listen. I think I'm gonna go check out that social media promo you told me about and then head to bed. Things start early around here."

Jane let out a huff. "I'm so jealous of you. I miss the excitement of being on a set. I'm bored to death working at a desk in an office all day."

"Hey, at least you got a job right away. That's a good thing."

"Yeah, I'm grateful. And I really am happy for you that you got the new show, but I'm still reserving the right to be envious once in a while."

Tasha smiled, not forgetting that in spite of her issues with her co-host she was damned lucky to be working at all herself. "All right. I'll allow it. Okay, let me go. I'll call you soon."

"You'd better. Have a good night with Mr. Hottie."

That was probably the worst idea Jane had ever had. "Good night, Jane," Tasha said.

She disconnected the call before her friend could make any more comments about Clay's hotness.

Tasha didn't need any reminders about that. She knew first hand . . . literally. She'd had her hands all over him last night as she held on for dear life while he pounded her into multiple orgasms.

His male prowess wasn't the problem. Not at all.

It was everything else about the man that she took issue with. But definitely not the sex, because there was no doubt he was very good at *that*.

Cell in hand she shuffled to the kitchen in her PJs and flip-flops and headed for the tea kettle she'd bought at Home Depot when they'd been out shopping for tile. She'd remembered to pack her favorite herbal tea from home but hadn't considered there'd be nothing to boil water in.

Luckily, she wasn't as neat and tidy as she should be and there was a to-go mug still sitting in her car's cup holder from before production had started. It was a good thing she'd forgotten to take that into her condo because now she had something besides a paper cup in which to drink her tea.

As she filled the kettle with water she realized she was pretty good at this roughing it stuff. Just as good as Clay was. Better, in fact, since she wasn't sneaking out into civilization to do who knew what every night.

Ha! In the battle of the co-hosts, she was clearly the winner.

Smiling, she picked up her phone. She had a bit of time to kill waiting for the water to boil so she navigated to her Facebook app.

Time to find the show's page and this new video and see what the hell the producers had created without telling her. Then, when Clay finally did come back, she could tell him about how the studio was already posting video of him on the show.

That should really piss him off. It would serve him right for sneaking off to . . . to . . . wherever.

Humph. That bastard had better not have a girlfriend, strictly because she didn't like the idea of being the other woman. No other reason, of course. She wasn't jealous or anything. Definitely not.

She sighed and glanced at the kettle, wishing it would boil. If ever she needed the calming effects of that herbal tea, it was now.

CHAPTER NINETEEN

Clay didn't know how many miles he ran along the water. He was going to have to drive the distance in the truck and check the odometer to find out. All he knew was he ran until his muscles and his lungs burned before turning around and making the long trip back.

His legs felt like gelatin and he had to have sweated out a gallon of water. Perfect. That ensured he was good and exhausted and not even thinking about fucking by the time he came in the back door of the house from the beach.

He kicked off his sandy sneakers just inside the door and wiped the sweat from his face with the T-shirt he'd pulled over his head. He tossed that onto the floor next to the sneakers.

In the morning, he'd discover if the washer and dryer that came with this place worked or not.

Tonight he was too damn tired to do laundry. Rehydration and a shower were the only things on his agenda.

He was heading into the kitchen to handle the first item on his to-do list when he saw Tasha already inside and stopped dead in the doorway. She was in the same outfit as last night, standing and staring at the teakettle on the burner.

On the counter next to the stove were a cup and a box of tea.

Who drank hot tea in this weather? Also, when the hell had they gotten a teakettle? Or a travel mug. Or, for that matter, tea bags?

He'd better pay more attention to what she was buying when they were out shopping for house stuff. She was probably tossing all sorts of random shit into the cart that he ended up paying for.

All those thoughts fled as he took one more sweeping glance at her and his gaze stalled on the pajama bottoms. Then the only thought he could focus on was peeling them off and plunging inside her.

The tight little tank top that she obviously didn't ever wear a bra with wasn't helping the situation either.

"Where were you?" she asked, looking him up and down with as much scrutiny as he'd given her seconds ago.

He was drenched in sweat and he'd come in through the door that led to the beach. Where the hell did she think he'd been?

"I was out taking dance lessons." He rolled his eyes. "Not that it's any of your business, but I went for a run on the beach."

She scowled but didn't comment. Instead she started playing with the phone in her hand.

He decided it was now his turn to question her. "Don't you own any other clothes to sleep in?" he asked.

She frowned. "Yes, but it's hot in here and these are the coolest ones I brought with me."

If it was so hot, she shouldn't be drinking frigging hot tea. Keeping that comment to himself, he scowled and walked away from her, heading toward the fridge.

What more could he say? He really shouldn't complain about what she wore. It wasn't like she was in slinky lingerie. She wore cotton pants that were way too big for her. The damn things shouldn't be sexy. But fuck it all, on her, paired with that tight little tank top, the outfit was tempting as hell.

"Don't you own a shirt?" she said to his back.

Indeed he was shirtless, but he was also in his own damn house, which was allowed if not expected. But apparently this was the best comeback she could think of.

As he twisted off the cap on a bottle of water, he turned to face her. He didn't miss how she had been staring at his back—and now his front—before her cheeks turned pink and she yanked her gaze up to his face.

Smiling, he took a long swallow and shook his head. "Nope. Us *cavemen* don't wear shirts. We only wear loincloths."

Eyes wide, she sucked in a breath. "Oh my God. You read my journal."

It had been an accident, but yes he had. And all the adolescent insults aimed at him that she'd scrawled on the one page he'd skimmed before tossing it back down and going on with his day had only made him laugh out loud.

The damn thing read like a prepubescent girl having a hissy fit, right down to the best line, where she'd called him a *stupid mean caveman*.

He'd been holding on to the tidbits he'd read all day, waiting for the best time to use them against her. Tonight, after her ridiculous shirt comment, seemed like the perfect time.

Clay cocked a brow. "Don't leave it laying around if you don't want me to read it. Besides, I thought it was your house notebook."

She planted her hands on her hips as her mouth twisted in ugly satisfaction. "I thought you said my renovation notebook was stupid."

He wasn't about to admit to her the damn notebook had been useful, that one time at least. "It is stupid. But I needed the measurement for the space between the toilet and the tub and you were hogging the bathroom at the time—as usual."

She let out a *humph*.

"You know, if you don't want me to write how you're a caveman, perhaps you shouldn't act like one." She paused for a second then drew in a breath before continuing, "And cavemen don't wear loincloths. *Tarzan* wears a loincloth. Cavemen wear— I don't know—like toga thingies made out of wooly mammoth skins or something."

His lips twitched in spite of himself. She really did like to hear herself talk, but he had to admit— although never to her, of course—her rambling could be kind of cute at times.

When she finally stopped babbling to take a breath, he asked, "Are you done?"

Eyes narrowed, she bit her bottom lip and he had to force his gaze off her mouth and the accompanying fantasy of what it would look like wrapped around his cock.

Finally, she said, "Maybe."

"Good." He spun on the tile floor in his sweaty socks and padded out of the kitchen, saying as he walked, "I'm taking a shower."

"Fine, but don't hog the bathroom for too long."

He smiled again until he noticed his cock was already at half mast just from their bickering.

This damn woman was going to be the death of him.

CHAPTER TWENTY

The lukewarm shower followed by a blast of cold water cooled his overheated body and overactive libido nicely, even though he had opted to forgo *handling* things himself. The walls in this house were, as he'd already learned, too damn thin.

He should insulate. Provide some soundproofing. But that was a lot of work and expense for nothing since in less than three and a half weeks he'd have his privacy back. He could whack off whenever or wherever he wanted then.

For now, he'd just have to deal with it—and with her.

At least he was cooled off and clean, if not satisfied.

Thinking two out of three wasn't bad, Clay stepped out of the tub and reached for a towel. He ran it over his head, getting most of the water out of his hair before he tossed it onto the rack and reached for his toothbrush.

He'd barely finished brushing his teeth when the soft knock came on the door.

Frowning, he glanced around him for something to put on, even though he knew what he'd find. His choices were sweaty shorts and underwear he had no intention of putting on his clean body, and the towel he'd just used.

Given those limited options he wrapped the towel around his waist, tucked in the end to secure it at his hip and pulled open the door.

Tasha stood there, wide-eyed as her gaze dropped to his state of undress. Her cheeks colored as she yanked her eyes back up to meet his. That's what she got for disturbing him in his own bathroom.

"Yes? Can I help you?" he asked, his hand still on the door as he blocked the entrance.

She held up the cell in her hand as if that would explain the need for this interruption. It didn't. What was she trying to say in this bad game of charades?

"Can I come in?" she finally asked.

He lifted a brow and glanced at the steamy room he had no desire to be confined inside with her. "Why?"

"I need to show you something." She pushed past him without invitation.

He closed the door once she was inside. He might be unhappy about this turn of events but he wasn't stupid. This room was their sole sanctuary and the door its only defense against the cameras.

There was definitely something upsetting her. He glanced at the cell in her hand but couldn't see the screen. "What's wrong?"

Had she gotten bad news? Had the show been canceled before it even aired?

Thank God he'd nixed Joanne's initial offer that the show buy the house and he purchase it from them after production at their cost. He didn't trust Hollywood folks as far as he could throw them. He'd stuck to his ground and the house was in his name and his alone so he'd be fine if the show was shut down.

Tasha, however, would be out of a job. That could explain the look on her face.

"I had nothing to do with this. I swear. I didn't even know it was up until Jane called me."

Who the fuck was Jane? And what was she babbling about? "Tasha, what are you talking about?"

With a huff, she thrust her cell at him again. There was a video cued up. He glanced at her, still confused.

"Hit play," she said, as her gaze skipped away from his.

What was on here that she couldn't even look him in the eye?

He looked back to the screen. Her cell was one of those huge overpriced ones he'd never own until they started giving them away free.

It was like a tiny television in his hand so he could see clearly the *play* button. He hit it with one finger and the sound came blaring out as the picture was set in motion.

He heard music, and then a narrator as the show logo filled the screen. Then it was him on the web, close up and in living color. And of course, there was Tasha too.

The video was a minute and a half of him and her fighting with each other, only it didn't look anything like what had happened in real life. And he'd been there so he knew.

Instead, they'd edited it so their bickering came across more like foreplay in a bad movie. He was in the role of the grunting workman, opposite Tasha as the bitchy housewife he'd have to tame.

The whole thing was so ridiculous he let out a laugh.

Finally, the show graphic and the narrator was back saying, *"Home renovation has never been hotter. Hot House coming this September."*

"Wow." Shaking his head, he handed the phone back to her and saw her stricken expression.

"I'm so sorry," she said.

"What are you sorry about?" he asked.

"About that. That they posted it and didn't get our approval. The way they edited it . . ." She shook her head looking distraught.

He laughed again. "Tasha, you've been in this business longer than me but even I know they're going to do whatever the hell they want, with or without our permission. I knew what I was signing up for. I just can't believe they actually managed to twist us arguing all day into *that*. It's ridiculous."

"It's not totally ridiculous," she hissed low in a whisper. "Clay, what if they heard us in here together? Or compared the camera feeds and figured out we were both in here at the same time? They could know and that's why they edited that video like that."

He shook his head. "No."

"Don't say no. It's possible." Her voice held a tinge of panic as it got louder.

"Check what time that video was posted." He tipped his chin toward the cell in her hand. "It was posted yesterday morning. Hours before we—you know."

Her focus whipped to the screen and she visibly let out a breath of relief.

"You knew Maria was going to play up how we always disagree on everything since she sent us that video from the tile aisle and told us to fight more," he reasoned.

"I know, but I didn't think they were going to spin it to be so . . . *sexual*," she hissed the last word in a loud whisper. "And when I saw that posted, right after what we did, I thought . . ."

"I understand, but you saw the time stamp. They don't know and *that* . . ." He tipped his head toward the sink, the scene of their sexual crime. ". . . is *never* going to happen again, so we're fine. Right?"

Lips pressed tightly together, she nodded.

"Right. We're fine. Never gonna happen again." She raised her gaze to his face, but not before skimming over his towel-draped hips and bare chest. "Sorry I bothered you."

"It's all right. Thanks for telling me about the video." Now he was prepared for the razzing he'd get if any of the guys found it.

"No problem." She swallowed hard and glanced at the door. "I guess I'll head to bed."

He tipped his head. "Good night."

"Good night." With one more glance back at him she reached for the doorknob and slipped out into the hall, closing the door behind her.

He braced both palms against the sink and looked at his reflection in the mirror. Two nights of crap sleep showed clearly beneath his eyes and he had a feeling tonight wasn't going to be much better.

Three and a half more weeks. He'd just have to keep repeating that to himself. He'd get through this one day—and night—at a time, just like how he'd survived Hell Week during BUD/S.

Retirement wasn't supposed to be this hard.

Of course, he'd never planned his retirement to include Tasha Jones and the cameras that came with her.

With a sigh, he gathered up his dirty clothes from the floor and headed for his lonely bedroom.

CHAPTER TWENTY-ONE

"Why don't you have a girlfriend?" Tasha hadn't meant to ask it, but it slipped out.

Apparently she had no control of herself when she was anywhere near Clay. Not in the bathroom. Not at breakfast.

He'd obviously been out running last night, just as he'd said, but she still wasn't convinced he didn't have someone in his life he was hiding from the cameras. It would explain why he'd vowed they'd never repeat that one night in the bathroom.

She wasn't bold enough to ask if he had a girlfriend, so she'd broached the subject in a bit more roundabout way.

His gaze whipped up to meet hers before it cut to the cameraman hovering nearby.

Okay, in hindsight she had to admit it was probably a bad idea to start this conversation with the cameras around. It probably should have been held in the bathroom at night, but it was too late to take it back now.

He frowned and asked, "Why don't you have a

boyfriend?"

Tasha scowled at his avoidance of the question and how he'd turned it back on her. "I asked you first."

Clay blew out a breath as the furrow grew deeper between his brows. He was definitely not happy with her.

He was silent for long enough she thought he might not answer. Not even looking at her, he remained hunched over his breakfast sandwich like it was the best meal he'd ever eaten, rather than mass-produced and wrapped in paper.

Finally, he said, "My career made having a serious relationship difficult."

"Your career in the Navy?" she asked.

After he leveled an angry glare at her, he shot another glance at the cameraman and said, "Yes."

"Were you deployed a lot?" she asked.

His eyes widened. The man's emotions were an open book, clearly written all over his face, and what she read told her he didn't like this conversation.

Why? It was an innocent enough topic. She was just trying to fill some dead air as they sat and ate before starting the workday.

"You didn't answer my question." He stared at her, waiting, as if daring her to not answer after she'd pushed him to.

"I was concentrating on my career. I didn't have time to date." Tasha shrugged but wasn't ready to let his cagey answer go without a follow-up. "You don't like talking about your time in the Navy, do you?"

"Not true." He glanced up at her from below dark brows drawn low. "I don't like talking at all."

He went back to focusing on devouring his second

Sausage McMuffin while she had yet to get through half of her yogurt and granola parfait.

This conversation was going nowhere, as usual. He was closed off, distant and cold. Nothing like the man he'd been when he'd burst into the bathroom and rocked her body like it had never been rocked before.

He must really hate the cameras. Or maybe, sex aside, he just really hated her. But that other night . . . That night he'd made her believe there was something deeper there between them.

She nearly laughed at that. There had been something deep between them all right—his cock, buried deep in her. She needed to remember it was just sex. Nothing else.

None of that mattered anyway, or at least it shouldn't, because the only thing that was important in her life right now was making sure this show was a success.

Still, the man was a mystery that he could look at her with such heat at night and then with such heated disdain during the day.

Fine. She was feeling no love lost toward him this morning either. Maybe they were more alike than she thought.

Tasha shifted gears before Maria lost her mind that they were eating in silence. "We should move in some stuff for the kitchen and cook breakfast here ourselves instead of getting takeout every morning. It would be much healthier."

"Go for it. Buy whatever you want, but send the bill to your boss over there. I'm not bankrolling your healthy eating." Clay tipped his head toward Maria.

Tasha cringed. Not only had he been rude, Maria hated when he acknowledged the crew. They, like the cameras, were supposed to be invisible. Non-existent. So the viewer forgot they were there.

She'd heard other reality show stars say they eventually forgot the cameras were there after awhile. That had yet to happen for them on this show. Clay broke the rules and talked to or about the crew every chance he got. The editors were going to have a hell of a time cutting all of it out.

But back to his answer . . . she'd figured he'd want to start moving some of his own stuff in since they'd basically finished work on the kitchen.

"We probably don't have to buy anything new." She frowned. "Don't you own anything yourself?"

"Sure, I do."

That was a relief. He must have all his belongings in storage because there was nothing here at the house except for his seemingly bottom-less duffle bag that yielded an endless supply of T-shirts and shorts and not much else. She was beginning to believe he'd been homeless before the show.

"Okay. That's good. What do you have?" she asked, her notebook in hand so she could make a list of what they'd need to pick up.

"A surfboard. Two, no three deep sea fishing poles. A weight set. My grandfather's rifle. Ammo, of course. A tent. Um . . . Oh, and my knives." Apparently finished, he took another bite of his sandwich.

Given that list, she had a feeling he wasn't talking about cooking knives. She sighed. "So no pots and pans?"

"Nope. But I do seem to have somehow acquired a tea kettle." Even the smile he flashed her seemed to have its own bad attitude.

How could a man who had her writhing with pleasure at night be such an ass by the light of day? That wasn't a problem she could solve, but the cookware issue was.

"I'll go get some stuff from my place for us to use."

He lifted his shoulder. "Whatever floats your boat, sweetheart."

Tasha resisted the urge to look at Maria and see how this conversation was going over with her. Instead, she moved on to the day's work still ahead of them. "So, we're going to choose the living room and hallway paint colors today, right?"

"*I* am going to. Yeah."

She narrowed her gaze at him. "I'm coming with you."

"I'm making the choice," he shot back.

How were they back right where they'd started days ago? Arguing over everything.

What an ass.

She let out a breath. "Fine. Yes. As always you get the final choice. But can we at least bring home some samples and try out some colors other than white. Just like we did with the tile?"

He raised his gaze to shoot her a glare. He didn't have to say the words. They were clear in that one glance. He wasn't going to put up with her throwing it in his face that she'd been right about the blue glass subway tile.

Whatever. She'd keep her mouth shut, but when it turned out that he liked her color choices better than whatever boring old one he chose, she'd still get to feel justified, even if she couldn't say it aloud.

"So we'll head to the Sherwin Williams store right

after breakfast."

Frowning, he glanced up again. "That's twenty minutes away. We can just go to Home—"

Tasha opened her eyes wide hoping Clay would read her meaning and remember that Sherwin Williams had just joined on as a major sponsor and that a certain other large chain store was not to be mentioned on camera.

After a second, his brows lifted and an expression of recognition crossed his face. "Oh. Okay."

With a loud exhale, he gathered up his sandwich wrapping into a ball and tossed it into the garbage bin that had become the only other living room furnishing besides the folding table and chairs.

"Ready?" he asked, eyeing her still half-filled cup.

With a sigh, she put down her plastic spoon and reached for the lid. The rest could wait in the fridge. Time for them to go fight over paint colors.

She stood. "Ready."

Passionate at night. Pig headed by day. How could she want to sleep with him just as much as she wanted to slap him?

Living with Clay was certainly proving to be an adventure and a mystery.

CHAPTER TWENTY-TWO

In spite of the strange yearning arguing over paint colors with Clay had created inside her, Tasha made it through another night without giving in to the urge to break out B.O.B., but only because of the bedroom cameras and the knowledge the walls in this place were laughably thin. But there were many more nights of frustration ahead of her.

Luckily another workday had begun. While she was busy with production during the day she was fine. It was those long nights alone in her tiny bedroom that proved to be a problem.

Tasha sighed. One day at a time . . .

About mid-morning, they sat around the table in the living room for a quick production meeting—Maria, Tasha and of course Clay, who gripped a bottle of water in one fist and looked unhappy to be there.

She looked a little closer at him. Judging by the dark circles beneath his eyes, he wasn't sleeping that great either. That made Tasha feel moderately better.

Maria read the schedule aloud from the screen of her iPad Pro. "Tomorrow the painters will be here—"

"Wait." Clay frowned. "Tomorrow is Sunday."

Maria eyed him. "Yes. And?"

"You got a paint crew to work on a Sunday?" Clay asked.

She smiled. "Of course, we did. The show pays well and it's free advertising for the business. The owner told me he got new matching shirts for the crew printed with the company's name and phone number on them. Even if he does have to pay more to get his crew to work on a Sunday, it'll be worth it for the publicity. He's not stupid."

Clay scowled. "No, he's not. But I guess I am for assuming we'd have a day off during this thing."

"There's only three weeks left and there's a lot to get accomplished."

"I understand that. But most people have a day or two off a week," he grumbled.

Tasha watched the debate and sipped the iced coffee one of the assistants had delivered to her. It was interesting to be an observer in a fight that involved Clay and not her for once.

"You were in the Navy." Maria pointedly dropped her gaze to Clay's U.S. NAVY tattoo, visible on his forearm. "Didn't you work long hours and go a few weeks without a day off during your service?"

He scowled at that. "Yes. But—"

Maria's only reply as she waited for him to continue was one raised brow.

Clay stopped at the sight of her unyielding expression and blew out a breath. "I can be here in the morning but I can't work late the way we usually do. I need the evening off."

"What time?" Maria asked.

"I need to leave before seventeen-hundred—I

mean five p.m.," he corrected himself while Tasha tried to ignore the flutter in her groin his slip into military-speak had caused.

She'd lived in this area for five years and had never dated a sailor. Who knew she had a thing for military men? Certainly not her . . . and not until now. Until him.

Ugh, were they all hot as hell and stubborn as a jackass? And why was she so physically, irresistibly, attracted to him?

Supposedly women got turned on by their brains first and their bodies second. She'd always gone for guys who were smart and funny, not pig-headed Neanderthals like Clay.

Though maybe that was the answer right there. Her biological clock must be ticking and some instinct left over from the caveman days of humanity was tricking her body into thinking Clay would make a good mate.

She had no doubt he would. If killing wooly mammoths to put food on the fire and fathering their own clan of cave babies were the only issues, then Clay would be a perfect mate.

But as a match for a modern woman? Not so much.

Meanwhile, while Tasha had been occupied considering Clay's caveman abilities and attributes, the battle between him and Maria was still going.

Maria scrolled through her tablet and finally nodded. "Fine. You can leave at five. The painting crew and Tasha can continue without you. I can leave the main crew here and send just a cameraman with you to wherever—"

"No." His single word was loud and firm.

"Clay—"

"Maria. No! I've put up with a lot. I've let you invade my privacy and my home and even my damn bedroom, but the line I draw is here. No camera. Not for this."

"And what exactly is *this*?" Maria asked as Tasha wondered the same thing.

"It's private." Clay held up his hand when Maria opened her mouth to protest. He shook his head. "I'm serious. This is a deal breaker for me."

His expression looked deadly serious. Tasha had seen him annoyed and angry, but she'd never seen such focused unwavering determination in him.

Would he really walk away from this deal and this house and be in breach of contract for one camera-free evening?

As she watched his nostrils flare while he glared at Maria, unflinching, Tasha had a feeling he might.

For some strange reason she couldn't figure out, Tasha wanted to help him. Maybe because for once it didn't seem like he was being contrary on purpose. Whatever he had to do, it was important to him.

She had an idea. "You know, Maria, I think it might be kind of fun to be on set alone for a few hours without Clay. I can play up how now that he's not here I can make all the decisions on my own. Maybe I'll even bring out a can of pink paint and threaten to paint his bedroom that color as a joke. It'll be funny."

Maria drew in a breath and finally broke eye contact from the staring contest she'd been having with Clay. Her focus moved to Tasha.

"I think that might work." She turned her gaze back to him. "Clay?"

"Fine." He didn't even balk about the pink paint idea proving this thing, whatever it was, was big. That only made Tasha want to know what it was even more.

Was Jane's guess right? Did Clay secretly have a girlfriend? Was this mystery event he couldn't miss some sort of date? And if he'd go to so much effort to be with this girl on this particular day, why the hell had he screwed Tasha on the bathroom sink?

Her stomach twisted at the thought.

She glanced in his direction. Jaw clenched, breathing fast, brows drawn low, Clay was visibly agitated. The man's emotions showed clearly on his face, but he was still a closed book when it came to her trying to read his thoughts and his motivations.

What was Clay's deal? She was angry with herself for even wondering, but far more disappointed that she cared. That she couldn't fight the attraction, in spite of it all.

"All right. That's what we'll have to do then." Maria blew out a breath as she tapped on her iPad's screen. "Tomorrow, Clay will leave at five and Tasha, the crew and the painters will stay here and keep working with the cameras rolling."

Maria didn't look happy with the plan. Neither did Clay, even if he had gotten his way.

Tasha wasn't all that satisfied with this outcome either. All it had done was make her wonder what Clay was up to.

She hated nothing more than an unsolved mystery . . . so perhaps she should do something about solving this one.

It was definitely something to think about.

CHAPTER TWENTY-THREE

McP's was abuzz by the time Clay walked in.

The guys already had a table and a round of drinks in front of them. No surprise. They'd planned to meet at seventeen-thirty and Clay had walked in at seventeen-twenty, but he knew his friends and had no doubt they'd all gotten there early.

Asher only had to drive from the base, which was barely a stone's throw away. The others had driven or flown in specifically for this. It was that important to them all—and he'd nearly been late because of a fucking reality show.

Jaw clenched from residual anger over the whole debate with Maria that had nearly kept him away, Clay glanced behind him one more time. It didn't hurt to be extra careful.

He'd kept one eye on his rear-view mirror the whole drive over to make sure she hadn't put a camera crew on him. He could spot a tail better than most, and he didn't think some Hollywood production company would have cameramen who even knew how to follow someone unobserved, so he was probably safe.

So far, so good. He hadn't spotted anyone on the road and he didn't notice anyone here now.

If she had sent a crew to follow him, he would have turned the truck around and missed this rather than have it tainted. His teammate Randy had sacrificed himself to save the rest of the team five years ago to the day. He deserved better than to have his memorial be exploited for television ratings.

"Dirtman." Asher had spotted him from across the bar and waved him over.

No need. Clay had seen them the moment he'd walked in, in spite of the fact they'd chosen the darkest, farthest, most secluded corner in the place. He'd just been avoiding going over until he was sure the coast was clear.

He moved over now, catching Raymond's eye and holding up one finger to the bartender as he walked by.

Ray would know what he wanted. They'd been meeting here and ordering the same drinks on the same night every year for five years now.

Clay spotted the usual cast of characters. Each had his cocktail of choice on the table in front of him.

His gaze landed on the empty chair with the full shot glass sitting in front of it. He tipped his head toward the vacant place and the untouched shot, acknowledging the teammate who was there in spirit but not body.

He could picture Randy downing those damn Blowjob shots like it was yesterday, rather than half a damn decade ago.

The man ordered them like they were candy. Hell, they might as well be candy since they were made out of all sweet shit and cream. The big Texan didn't care about the girly ingredients in his drink of choice and no one would have ever dared comment on it anyway. Well, no one outside of his brothers on the team. From them, Randy got plenty of shit.

Clay forced his gaze off that shot and empty chair and moved to the next table over where a man and a woman sat at a table with three seats. "Anyone using this?" he asked, resting his hand on the back of the empty chair.

The guy, who had Navy written all over him, shook his head. "Nope. It's all yours."

"Thanks, man." Clay swung the chair around and shoved it in the narrow space between Asher and Chase Flannigan.

"I was worried you weren't gonna make it." Asher, smartass to the core, waggled his eyebrows. "Thought you might be too busy with . . . other things."

"Fuck off, Knots." Clay rolled his eyes. "I'm not late."

Chase *tsked*. "Now, Dirtman, you know what the commander always said."

"If you're not early, you're late." The commander in question, Connor "Hammer" Evans, raised his glass in a toast to Clay.

"I know. I know." Clay shook his head, accepting the criticism.

His former teammates hadn't signed their lives away to a devil corporation from Hollywood with enough lawyers to sink Clay if he didn't toe the line. However, that was not a subject he planned to discuss here and now with these guys.

"So, how's the TV show going?" Asher asked.

Or maybe he was.

He braced for the onslaught of questions and jokes and wasn't disappointed. It was like Asher had dumped a bucket of bloody chum in the water and his teammates were the sharks riled into a feeding frenzy.

The questions came fast and furious. Too many to keep track of and answer in any cohesive order.

Clay held up one hand to silence them. "If everyone shuts up for a second, I'll explain."

He glanced behind him to see where his drink was and spotted it sitting on the bar waiting for a cocktail waitress to deliver it.

Waiting was not Clay's strong suit so he stood and stalked to the bar. He grabbed the martini and took a big sip before he carried it back to the table.

Setting down the glass, he took his seat again and drew in a breath. "All right. Here's what happened . . ."

The story he told was heavily edited. Clay played up how conniving the production company had been swooping in and driving up the price of his house. He made sure they knew how perfect it was and how he had to do something—anything—to make sure it was his. And he mentioned Tasha as little as he could get away with, all while shooting Asher repeated warning glances to tell him to keep his mouth shut.

When he was finally done, the guys sat silent—a rarity.

Finally, Gunner said, "Wow. You lucky motherfucker. It just figures you retire and two months later you're a damn reality TV star."

"I'm nothing of the sort. It's on some cable channel I never heard of and believe me, if there were any other way for me to get that house I would have done it."

Nikko shrugged. "I don't know. It sounds kind of cool."

"You wouldn't think so if they had night-vision cameras running twenty-four/seven in your bedroom so they can capture every fucking thing you say or do even after the camera crew goes home."

Carson asked, "Hard-wired or wireless?"

"Wireless." Clay frowned as he grabbed on to what Carson was getting at even before he explained. It was like a light bulb went off in his head. "I can jam the signal."

Carson nodded. "Hell yeah, you can. All it takes is one little device."

"Shit. You're right." Why hadn't he thought of that sooner?

Because he was so out of his element in this world of TV he forgot one basic thing. He was a SEAL and a good one. His skills would work in the civilian world just as well as they did in the military. He just had to remember to apply them.

"Well now. This sounds like a fun mission. What are we going to call it? Operation Fuck with the Producers?" Asher rubbed his hands together in anticipation.

An alternate name popped into Clay's head, unbidden. *Operation Fuck the Co-Host.* In a real bed instead of against the bathroom sink, all without anyone hearing or seeing it on the camera feed.

But they'd agreed. They weren't going to do that again.

It had been a moment of weakness and insanity that had it happening the first time. It wasn't going to happen again.

But damn, with the jammer it would be so easy.

Next to him, Asher whipped out his cell phone, typed in a text and then stashed it again in the cargo pocket on his thigh before he glanced at Clay. "A jammer will be in your truck by the time you leave tonight."

"What? What are you talking about?" Clay frowned.

"I texted one of the new guys on the team. I told him to acquire a signal jammer and deliver it to your truck in the parking lot before nineteen-thirty."

"And he's going to do it?" Clay asked.

"Fuck yeah, he is. He so young and eager, he'll do whatever the hell I ask him to do." Asher grinned.

Clay laughed. Asher's deadline was only two hours from now. The kid would no doubt have to scramble to get it done.

"At least the fucking new guys are good for something." Trevor shook his head, a mug of black coffee in front of him on the table since he didn't drink.

"All we got is fucking new guys now that you sons of bitches left," Asher pointed out.

"Hey, Knots. Civilian life ain't too bad. You should try it." Nikko raised his beer to Asher.

Asher shook his head. "One day. But not today."

The conversation thankfully moved away from Clay's life and turned to other things, like what the other guys were up to.

It was good to catch up. He missed seeing his teammates on a daily basis. He'd spent more time over the last twenty years with them than he had with his own family.

Retiring and being separated from them was a drastic change in his life.

A change that big could mess with a man's mind. Maybe that was one reason why this house seemed so important to Clay. It wasn't life or death that he get it, but damn, it felt that way sometimes.

But it was good to be with his old teammates now. To forget, for a few hours at least, they would all go back to their separate lives tomorrow. To ignore that he might not see some of them again for another year, until they all met back here again for another toast to Randy. To forget that, for the guys like Asher who were still on active duty, one mission gone bad could mean he'd never see him again.

Clay reached for his glass, surprised to see it was almost empty. He glanced around and saw that save for Randy's still full shot, they all needed a refill.

"Another round?" he asked, though he knew the answer already.

A rousing response of *fuck, yeah* confirmed it.

Clay smiled as he pushed his chair back, liking the familiarity they all shared. For the first time since retiring, he felt like himself again.

Too bad the feeling wasn't going to last.

CHAPTER TWENTY-FOUR

"So I want a really pretty feminine color. Like lavender or a really soft rose." Tasha had trouble keeping a straight face as she explained what she wanted to the store employee helping her.

It would serve Clay right if she actually painted his bedroom pink or purple. But the following weeks of fallout and foul moods wouldn't be worth the five minutes of fun.

This whole trip to the paint store was just for show. A bit of humor thrown in to make Maria happy so Clay could go out tonight and do . . . whatever.

The man standing next to her frowned down at the color swatches in her hand before his gaze moved to her face. "This is for the same house you were here about earlier in the week?" he asked.

She nodded.

"Clay's house?"

"The *Hot House* show house," she corrected. "But yes. It's the house I'm working on with Clay."

She hated that in five minutes Clay and the paint store guy had bonded. It turned out they'd both been in the Navy, so of course the whole discussion had excluded her. It had been like watching *The Clay Show* and she was just the audience.

They'd barely remembered she was there and they certainly hadn't taken any of her suggestions seriously.

It was just her luck that the one time she got to come to the store alone, the same guy was working and he, of course, remembered Clay.

He knew damn well Clay would never approve of the colors she'd just suggested.

"Which room is this for?" he asked, still looking baffled.

"The master bedroom."

His eyes widened. "Clay's bedroom."

"Yes."

The man's mouth opened and closed again. "We sell sample sizes. You can bring home the colors and try them out on the wall."

He was too well trained to outright disagree with her but he was obviously trying to lead her away from making what he no doubt thought was a huge mistake.

She'd be really angry at that if she weren't pulling his leg to begin with by making those outrageous color suggestions for Clay's bedroom.

Tasha sighed. The sad part was, she felt to her core that a beautiful soft sea glass blue with white trim would be perfect in Clay's bedroom. He'd vetoed her suggestion immediately without even looking at the swatches she'd tried to show him. He wanted white.

White! Plain old boring white walls with white trim. She couldn't imagine anything less inspired . . . So why didn't she show him the error of his ways?

Tasha reached into her bag and pulled out her

house book. Flipping to the master bedroom section, she pulled out the color swatch she'd wanted from the beginning.

"What do you think of this one?" she asked.

He nodded. "I love it."

She nearly laughed. Compared to pink or lavender for a man's bedroom, of course the clerk would love blue.

Maybe she should take this tactic all the time. Suggest something outrageous and ridiculous first, and then after Clay was suitably shocked and appalled, bring out her real choice.

He might be so relieved he'd let her have her way. It certainly had worked out that way with the paint guy.

"So what do you think? The room's already been primed so one gallon of color for a hundred square foot room?"

He tipped his head again, no longer questioning her choice. "That should do it. Flat or eggshell?"

"Flat, I think. It'll hide any imperfections better, right?" she asked, since Clay had outright refused to strip the place to the beams and put up new sheetrock.

"Yup. You know your stuff," the man smiled.

"Thank you." She returned his smile.

He might be flattering her because she was a customer, or because the cameras were there, or possibly because he was flirting with her. It didn't matter why. She got next to no compliments from Clay, so she was going to enjoy getting one now.

Having Clay take the evening off was turning out to be a good thing.

As the man mixed the color, Tasha couldn't resist

one more dig at the absent Clay. "Hey, do you know if the garden center down the road has any of those pink plastic flamingos people put in their yards? I wanted to pick a couple up for the house to surprise Clay."

The salesman's eyes widened. "Um, I don't know."

Behind her, she heard the cameraman snort.

Smothering her own smile, she said, "That's okay. I'll just stop by on the way home."

Less than an hour later, two pink flamingos graced the small patch of yard right by the front door where Clay would be sure to see them whenever he rolled in tonight. And Tasha had the paint color she wanted for his bedroom.

She dropped off the gallon of blue wall color along with a gallon of semi-gloss white trim paint with the painting crew, who agreed to work until they got the room done tonight.

They said they planned to be finished and gone by eight that night, which was a good thing. She wanted the room painted and the painters gone before Clay came home from his mystery date. That way he couldn't stop them if he hated the color.

But more than that, she wanted the room complete and looking great so he could maybe, by some miracle, appreciate that she'd been right.

The blue and the white was the perfect choice for a beach house bedroom. And if he added white cottage-style bedroom furniture, and maybe even white interior plantation shutters on the windows—it'd be fabulous.

She needed to show him how good it could look if he'd just listen to her.

Maria had left for the day, so Tasha turned to her

cameraman. "What do you say we knock off early tonight? Clay's not here and the painters are going to work on their own without me so . . ."

Greg flipped a switch and lowered the ever-present camera from his shoulder. "Sounds good to me. See you in the morning." He turned and headed for the door.

That was easy.

Tasha waited for him to pull out of the driveway and then grabbed her own car keys. If he knew she was going out, he'd follow her—Maria's orders.

For what she had in mind, she didn't need a shadow. All she was going to do was run to her house and print out some stuff. If she left some pictures of her ideas for furnishings in Clay's room for him to find, he'd see she was right . . .

It wasn't a great plan but it was the only one she had. And while she was there, she could grab a few things she needed. She was already tired of the clothes she'd packed and they had weeks left of production.

She made a list in her head of what she wanted to take back to the house as she drove toward her condo but she didn't quite make it there as a thought struck her.

Where would Clay go on his night off? She only knew one place he might be, but she also knew for a fact he'd gone there two days in a row.

McP's.

What were the chances he was there now? She figured pretty good.

Swinging the car into a tight turn, she got on the road that would lead to McP's. She'd just drive by and see if his truck was parked there. Or maybe pop in for a quick drink and ask the bartender if he'd seen him, since Clay seemed to be on a first name basis with the guy.

Happy with this new plan, Tasha slowed as she neared the bar and—*son of a bitch*—there was Clay's big ass truck parked on the side street.

Heart beating faster, she swung her car into an empty space and threw it into park.

He had to leave early just to come to the bar? What the hell?

There were plenty of times she didn't feel like working a twelve-hour day, but she did it. Why was he special that he thought he didn't have to do the same?

She remembered how hard he'd fought Maria to get tonight off and how he'd reacted when she'd suggested putting a camera on him. Something besides his desire for a night off to get a beer was going on—and of course that had her thoughts circling back to the possibility there was a woman involved.

Pulse racing, she grabbed her bag, locked the car and headed for the door.

Inside, it didn't take her long to spot him. He was hard to miss, especially since he was standing at the bar.

Tasha strode up to him. "What are you doing?" she asked, though it sounded more like an accusation than a question.

His eyes widened. "What the fuck are you doing here?" His gaze moved past her, toward the door. "And please tell me you don't have a fucking camera on you."

"There's no camera. And why does it matter anyway if all you're doing is drinking? And you couldn't wait until after we were done for the day to do that?"

He sucked in a breath through his teeth. "You need to leave."

"Why?"

"Because there are parts of my life that don't concern you or this damn show, that's why." His eyes had an angry, crazed look about them. It might be scary if she weren't so annoyed.

"You signed away your privacy when you accepted the terms of that contract and the big old payout. Remember?"

The payout that matched hers, which was still completely unfair in her opinion.

"I might have signed away my rights, but that doesn't include the right to privacy for the people in my life."

"Ah ha! So that *is* it. Which one is she, Clay? Hmm?" Tasha fought the sick feeling of disgust in her gut with pure spiteful jealous rage. "I bet she'd be interested in knowing what you and I did the other night."

"Holy shit." He shook his head. "If you'd stop being such a bitch for a minute—"

"Bitch? That's the best you can come up with, Clay?" The insult to his intelligence didn't give her as much joy as it should have as tears pricked behind her eyes. Then they weren't behind her eyes any longer but instead cascading down her cheek.

"Fuck." Clay grabbed her arm and pulled her toward the door.

She tried to shake off his hold on her, but his grip was too tight. "Stop manhandling me."

"I'm not manhandling you. I'm trying to save both of us a lot of embarrassment."

"Why? Because your girlfriend is inside?" To her horror, her voice cracked on a sob.

Outside Clay backed her up against the wall. "Tasha, listen to me."

"No, you cheater."

He laughed, bringing her head up as confusion temporarily halted her tears. "I'm many things, but not a cheater."

"Liar *and* a cheater." She was rapidly losing her steam as hurt overwhelmed her.

He shook his head, smiling and confusing her more. "I don't have a girlfriend. I'm not seeing anyone, casually or seriously. In fact, you're the only person I've had sex with in more months than I'd like to admit. Happy?" he asked.

"I don't believe you." But boy did she want to.

"Why not?" he asked, still looking amused by her.

"You keep sneaking out at night."

"Once was to meet my buddy for a drink. My *guy* buddy who made enough fun of me for being a part of this damn show without me showing up at this bar with a camera up my ass. The second time was to take a run on the beach, just like I told you."

"And tonight?" she asked.

"Tonight was private." Finally, he drew in a breath. "A friend died five years ago today. Every year we get together to honor him. I didn't want the cameras here for that."

"Wow. Clay, I'm sorry. I didn't know."

"Because I didn't want anyone connected to the show to know."

"I'm not connected—" When he cocked his brow she clarified, "I mean I'm not a producer or a director. I'm in the same boat as you are. Just a co-host working at the whim of the production company. I want my privacy sometimes too. I would have understood you needing yours. For something like *this* especially."

He hesitated and then nodded. "You're right. I should have explained it to you."

"Thank you for admitting that and for telling me now. It means a lot."

Clay pressed his lips tight. "You didn't really paint my room pink, did you?"

"No. Not pink." She cringed and dared to glance up at him.

His eyes widened. "Jesus. What color did you choose?"

"You'll see. And I think you're going to love it. Seriously. Especially once I show you how it could look once the room is furnished."

"Furnished? It is furnished. There's a bed and a table. That's all I need."

"There's a mattress and box spring on top of a metal frame and a folding snack table as the nightstand. That is not furnished."

He rolled his eyes but he'd come around. She'd see to it. Slowly but surely she was wearing him down.

"So, were you really upset at the thought of me having a girlfriend?" he asked.

She glared at him. "Yes! I'm not going to be the other woman you're cheating on your girlfriend with."

"That the only reason?" he asked, smiling.

"Yes. Of course." She broke eye contact. "What other reason could there be?"

"I don't know."

A guy leaned out of the door and zeroed in on Clay. "Dirtman! Where are those drinks?"

"Shit. I was about to order them when—"

"When you got distracted. So I see." The guy stepped forward and extended his hand. "Hey. I'm Asher. You must be Clay's co-host and roomie."

"I am. Tasha Jones." She shook the guy's hand and marveled how Clay's friend was equally buff and gorgeous as he was.

Did hot guys hang around together? And how many more of them were there inside just like this one?

She'd clearly been hanging out at the wrong places. The day of her final show was the first time she'd been here. She'd come back the next day to retrieve her car and meet with the producer, but she never hung out there. That had clearly been a mistake.

"Nice to finally meet you, Tasha. Clay has told me all about you."

"He has?" She sent a shocked glance in Clay's direction.

He was shaking his head. "Knots . . ."

His friend grinned. "I'll let you two finish your conversation. Oh, and I ordered the round, so take as long as you need." He winked at Clay and grinned at Tasha before yanking open the door.

Tasha got a look at the back of his blue T-shirt. It said NAVY in big gold letters.

"Your friend's in the Navy like you were?" she asked.

"Um. Yup."

"And your other friend who died, was he in the Navy too?"

"Yes." Tight-lipped, Clay reached for her elbow and glanced past her at the street. "Where are you parked? I'll walk you to your car."

"Over there." She gestured in the general direction of where she'd parked, badly and crooked, when she'd abandoned her car near his truck to stalk inside to find him.

He walked her to her car and even played gentleman and held the door open for her, but he hesitated closing it after she'd gotten inside and buckled the seat belt. "Tash?"

"Yeah?"

"I'd appreciate it if you'd keep tonight to yourself. What you saw, who you met, what I told you—all of it. Just please don't tell Maria or the crew, okay?"

"Okay, but I don't understand why."

That he and his Navy friends all got together to celebrate a lost friend—Clay should be proud of that and it would make one hell of a story for the show.

It would go a long way to making Clay seem more human. The female viewers would all fall in love with him. The men in the audience would respect and admire him.

It seemed like a win-win for everyone for Clay to share that part of his life. The military past that he hid so well.

"I don't expect you to understand, but it's important to me. I know I have to be on camera, but they don't." He tipped his head toward the building. "And I'll do anything I have to, to make sure they're not."

There was nothing but sincerity, concern and determination in his gaze. He was serious.

Tasha didn't understand his reasons, but she had to honor them. "All right. I won't say a word. I promise."

"Thank you. And I'll uh, take a look at your

decorating ideas for the bedroom . . . and try not to freak out about whatever color you chose."

"Thank you. That's all I'm asking." She smiled. "See, all we have to do is each give a little. We get along pretty good when we try."

He blew out a breath. "Yeah. That's exactly what I'm afraid of."

She didn't have time to question Clay's odd comment as he slammed the car door and took a step back onto the curb. His gaze met hers briefly through the car window as he dipped his head before he turned and headed back toward the bar.

Clay Hagan was one strange man. But damn, he'd never seemed hotter than he did tonight. She still didn't understand why the argumentative asshole version of Clay turned her on, but this new compliant, vulnerable version of him, the one surrounded by his Navy buddies—*damn*—it was even more irresistible.

She'd better get back to the house fast and break out B.O.B. before Clay got home and she couldn't indulge in that one small bit of relief.

Tonight she certainly needed it.

CHAPTER TWENTY-FIVE

Sleep didn't come for Clay that night, but a text did.

He was wide awake at midnight—he knew because he'd checked the time on his cell just moments before—when he heard the phone vibrate on top of the folding table next to his bed.

Reaching for it, he read the screen.

I can't sleep.

It was from Tasha down the hall and obviously wide-awake just like he was.

He knew why he couldn't sleep. She was the reason he was up. Or at least the sexual frustration she caused in him was the excuse he used to explain to himself why he couldn't sleep. But what the hell was her problem?

Probably too much tea before bed. That was her fault, not his.

He needed sleep, dammit. Just weeks to complete the renovations from start to finish was an insane timeline to begin with, even without having her as a distraction, fighting with him during the day and keeping him awake all night.

And then tonight, her being nice and understanding when she'd found him and the team at McP's. He didn't need the confusion of her acting like a decent human added to what was already so confusing between them.

He needed her to be exactly who he'd thought she was in the beginning—a self-centered diva.

And he *really* didn't need her texting him in the middle of the night.

He typed in the only reply he could come up with.

What do you want me to do about it?

Just seconds after he hit send, while the cell was still in his hand, her answer flew onto his screen.

I don't know . . .

He frowned at her response, his brain filling in what she hadn't written. Those three dots said all sorts of things she hadn't.

What the hell? Was this some sort of textual booty call from down the hall?

Shit. His cock liked the idea of fucking her into slumber. It tented his shorts beneath the sheet, ready and raring to go, but this time his mind wasn't going along for the ride.

What had happened the other night could *not* happen again, if for no other reason than that it would play right into Maria's deviant sexual twist to promote the show.

Legally, they could do whatever they wanted with the footage, but he'd be damned if he made it easy for them.

Just close your eyes and try to sleep.

He hit send on the message and watched the screen until her reply appeared, just as he knew it would.

I did. It didn't work.

What the hell was he supposed to do to help her? He was no sleep therapist.

When he'd been in the SEALs, they'd hand out Ambien like candy so the team could sleep on the transport and be ready to go when their boots hit the ground.

At other times they were so exhausted, falling asleep was never an issue. But here and now, he didn't know what to tell her to get her to stop texting him—tempting him.

Tasha. PLEASE. Just try.

He was begging now. Begging her *not* to have sex with him. In all caps, no less. What had this woman done to him?

Turned his damn life upside down, that's what.

He remembered the signal jammer in his truck and a bad idea that sounded way too good hit him.

It would take just minutes to set it up and have all the privacy he wanted right there in his bedroom. Or in hers.

Dammit, that was tempting. He didn't want to be tempted.

Freaking Carson and his bright ideas and Asher and his new guy—it was obviously their fault he was even considering doing this.

Before she even replied to his last text, he typed in another one and hit send before he regained his sanity.

Give me a few minutes.

She replied fast.

K

It was just a single letter, but it changed everything.

Like it or not, they were going to do it again. Have sex. Probably more than once, if his lack of self control tonight was any indication.

Shit.

He cussed himself and Asher one more time as he swung his feet over the edge of the bed and slid them into his flip-flops. Grabbing his keys on the way out, he navigated to his truck by moonlight.

With the device hidden in his gym bag, Clay tried to look casual as he smuggled it inside in the middle of the night. He made a beeline for the bathroom— the one room where he could set up the device without being seen on camera.

As predicted, the jammer took no time to set up. Then he was standing in the bathroom staring at the *No Signal* alert on the cell phone in his hand, proving he'd effectively blocked all signals, their cell phones as well as the camera feed.

Good thing it was the middle of the night. With the houses set so closely together in this neighborhood, the neighbors bordering his property were within the device's fifty-meter range and would suffer its effects too.

He'd knocked out everything in the area just so he could have sex with Tasha. He obviously had a problem, but apparently that knowledge wasn't going to deter him.

All he had to do was walk to her door and knock. Then, no doubt, they'd fall into bed together.

Was that what he wanted? Fuck, yeah.

Was it smart? Hell, no.

Did he care? At the moment, no. He didn't care all that much.

He had a raging hard-on, the residual effects of a

few martinis in his system and the intimate knowledge from Randy's sacrifice that life was too damn short to not live it to the fullest while he had the chance.

Drawing in a breath, Clay reached for the doorknob but then turned back, opening the medicine cabinet instead. He grabbed one of the sponsor's condoms—then thought better of it and grabbed a second.

Hell, if he was going to make a bad decision, he might as well really enjoy it.

Steeling himself against the common sense that still nagged him, he was out the door, across the hall and knocking on Tasha's door before he could change his mind.

She pulled it open seconds later.

"Hi." Her eyes locked on his when she saw him standing in her doorway.

"Hi." He took a step forward, forcing her to take a step back.

She glanced up at the camera mounted in the corner of her room and then back to him, the question clear in her expression. He could see her trying to reason out why he was there in her room while the cameras were running.

"Is this about the paint color?" she asked.

"No, it's not about the freaking color." He scowled. Why would he choose midnight to come to her bedroom to argue about the damn paint? "And the camera is off, so you can stop looking at it."

"What do you mean the camera is off?" she asked.

He lifted one shoulder. "I took care of them all."

"How did you take care of them?" she parroted his words once again.

Clay lifted a brow. "Are you just going to repeat

everything I say, or are we going to take advantage of a night without Big Brother watching us?"

She glanced at the camera one more time, and then back at him, as if not believing it.

If she needed proof, he had proof. He pulled his cell out of his pocket and turned it to face her, showing her the display.

Eyes wide, she glanced down at her own cell and then back up at him. "What did you do?"

"Not much." He shrugged. "Just jammed the signal."

With a piece of *borrowed* high-tech military equipment that probably cost the Navy an arm and a leg.

"So the cameras . . ."

"Will show as off-line," he completed her sentence. "Maria will never know. The production company will think the signal was out for a couple of hours. By morning, when anyone checks, the cameras will be back up and running."

She laughed. "Oh my God. You're like some sort of evil genius."

"That might be the first compliment you've ever given me." He folded his arms and leaned back against the doorframe, enjoying her praise since it might never happen again.

"But how did you do it?" she continued to question when there were so many better things they could be doing in their limited window of privacy.

"I know how to do these kind of things." He shrugged.

"Is that what you did during your time in the Navy?" she asked. "Were you some sort of communications expert?"

"I did a lot of things." He sidestepped one more question, but this back-and-forth was getting old. Time to move on. "So, what are we going to do with our new found freedom?"

Her gaze zeroed in on the hand where he still palmed the two condoms. "What's that?"

"Um . . . nothing?" For the first time tonight, Clay started to doubt his assumption about her intentions when she'd decided to text him from her bed in the middle of the night.

He'd expected to have a hand full of hot willing woman the moment he'd stepped into her room. Instead, this long-ass conversation had thrown him. Made him doubt himself. Her. Everything.

He must have misread Tasha. She could have texted him because she really couldn't sleep and wanted to talk about paint or something else equally ridiculous.

Shit. Had he somehow entered the friend zone by sharing just a small part of his life with her at the bar tonight? And here he stood, like a hopeful teenager with a fist full of condoms, about to get shot down.

She grabbed his hand in both of hers and pried his fingers open to reveal the protection he had thought was a good idea to bring with him.

A smile bowed her lips when she saw what he held, before she fisted his tank top and pulled him down toward her.

All righty, then. So he hadn't misinterpreted her signals. Good to know. And about damn time too. He'd had enough of this dancing around what she wanted.

Now that he knew for sure, he wasn't going to waste any more time. He hauled her against him and crashed his mouth over hers.

It seemed he couldn't take things slow or gentle when it came to this woman. It didn't matter if they were fighting or fucking, with her everything was hard and fast. He went all out and all in. And right now, he needed to be in her.

As she backed toward the bed and pulled him with her, he figured she was on board with that plan.

He ran his hands over the curve of her hips and around to the globes of her incredible ass.

The fabric covering her was smooth beneath his fingers. He broke the kiss and glanced down to get a look at the silky shorts covering her lower body.

The corner of his mouth quirked up in a smile. "So you do have other clothes to sleep in."

And these were even sexier than the last. Good thing he'd given up on resisting the temptation, at least for tonight. Tomorrow, when the mistake he was about to make was illuminated by the glaring light of day, he'd reevaluate the situation.

"Mmm, hmm. I snuck home and grabbed some things after I left McP's."

He feigned shock. "What? Without a camera crew with you? That's against Maria's rules."

"Yup. I told them I was going to bed early so I'd be out of the painting crew's way, and then I snuck out. I learned that little trick from you."

He was somehow managing to carry on a conversation while his cock strained the fabric of his shorts. "Glad I could teach you something. Get ready for another lesson."

Clay lifted her and tossed her onto the mattress. The bed frame creaked from his weight as he followed her down.

Her satiny little shorts were nice, but it was time they came off. He slipped his fingers beneath the elastic waist and yanked them down the legs he'd enjoy wrapped around him shortly—around his head first and then his waist later.

Perfect plan.

Intending to take advantage of the fact they were in a bed this time and not up against the bathroom sink, Clay slid down, spreading her thighs as he went. She watched him from beneath hooded lids as her breath came fast and shallow.

This woman fought hard, about everything to do with this house and the show, but he knew that when it involved sex, she also came hard. That was enough to make him do now what he knew he'd regret tomorrow morning.

Even as he leaned low and pressed a kiss to the inside of her warm thigh, his brain shouted that this was a bad idea.

All of it.

Indulging in a woman who should have been a one-night stand and instead had become a two-week one, so far.

Getting physically involved with someone he had nothing in common with, no future with, and who was also the person he worked with daily and should be maintaining a professional relationship with. Someone he fought with more than any other person in his life. Who made him so angry he could feel his blood pressure rise, yet who made him abandon all self-control and common sense when it came to her body.

Mixing business with pleasure was bad enough, but the most dangerous of all was that they were coworkers in one of the most public venues he could imagine.

He shouldn't be touching her at all, never mind have his head buried between her legs while he envisioned being ball's deep inside her in a few minutes, all while the house was full of cameras and the crew would be back in just hours.

Bad decisions, all of them—but damn it was good feeling her start to shake beneath him as he worked her with hand and mouth. He not only felt, but also heard the results as her orgasm broke and she came hard and loud.

Thank God for the signal jammer because every camera in the house definitely would have picked up the uncontrolled sound of her pleasure had they been hiding in the bathroom for this.

Screw the cameras. Screw the show. Bad decision or not, he'd started this thing and he intended to enjoy it and her.

With a groan of anticipation in his throat and the taste of her still on his tongue, Clay pulled himself up her body.

He rolled to the side long enough to kick his own shorts off his legs and onto the floor, then he felt for the condom packets he'd dropped on the bed sometime during this encounter.

His hand struck on one and he sat up on his knees between her spread legs as he sheathed himself.

She was still breathing heavily as he lifted her legs, lined himself up and plunged inside as she gasped.

His eyes slammed shut when her tight heat surrounded him. He cursed out loud as he feared the sensation would unman him and have him coming faster than a teenager.

Shaking with the effort, he tried to control the speed of his thrusts all while concentrating on not coming too soon.

It was hard, particularly with Tasha making all of those tiny—and some not so tiny—sounds that cut straight through him.

Her nails digging into his ass didn't help his concentration either. And then when she started to come, and bit his chest as she did, he was a goner.

He shot into her like a fifty caliber machine gun. Fast, powerful and he didn't stop until he was empty.

Trying and failing to support himself after the climax that drained him, he collapsed on top of her.

Not even a minute had passed, during which he spent his time trying to regain his breath while attempting to not completely crush her beneath him, when Tasha said, "So you never told me. Do you like the color of your room?"

Tasha's question was muffled, muted by his body on top of hers.

Clay let out a breathless laugh. "You want to talk about paint color now?" He was still semi-hard inside this woman and she was worrying about the renovation?

"Yes. I've been dying to know what you think. I've been waiting to ask you all night."

Clay shook his head, hating that she'd been thinking about paint while he'd been having what he considered some pretty great sex with her.

He hated what he was about to say even more than that, but he saw no way around it. "It's okay. I guess I can live with the color. But what the fuck are those pink things in my yard?"

"The flamingos were a joke, but don't try to

change the subject. I knew you'd like the blue once you saw it in the room." She looked too pleased with herself as she continued, "Wait until you see the pictures I printed out. And I also put together a Pinterest board of ideas. I can show you in the morning."

"Mmm, hmm."

"You're not even listening to me, are you?" She narrowed her eyes at him.

No, he wasn't listening. He was too occupied with how freaking amazing it felt to still be inside her.

"The question isn't why aren't I listening. It should be why are you talking?" He rocked his hips, thrusting with small slow movements as he grew hard again while inside her body.

She wasn't unaffected. Her lids drifted shut. With her mouth closed, she sucked in a ragged breath through her nose.

Much better.

He hooked a hand beneath the crook of her knee and lifted her leg, changing the angle of his stroke and causing her to gasp as he hit her G-spot.

The angle was doing some nice things for him too. "Damn, it's nice to do this in a bed."

"You're right. The bathroom last time . . . and I guess we did it on the sofa at my place that first night."

Uh, oh. Crap. He'd been lucky that so far the subject of that first night hadn't come up. And now he'd gone and inadvertently raised it himself and at the worst possible time.

But he couldn't lie to her now. Not while they were in the middle of doing what they were doing.

Pausing on the down stroke, Clay blew out a

breath and said, "About that first time. We, uh, never actually did anything that night."

"What?" If the palms she slapped against his chest hadn't told him she was unhappy with that revelation, the volume of her single word would have.

"What are you mad at me for? You're the one who passed out. Would you rather I have fucked you after you were out cold? I know you don't think much of me most days, but having sex with unconscious women is not an option for me."

"I passed out?" She frowned.

"Yes. Passed out. Fell asleep. I don't know which but one minute my hand was up your skirt and you sounded like you liked what I was doing, and the next you're limp and totally out of it."

"So what did you do?" she asked.

"I left."

The frown furrowing her brow deepened. "But wait. Then why when I saw you the next day at McP's you let me believe we'd had sex?" The anger was back in her voice mixed with a good bit of shock.

"Because you were siding with those house stealers and I was mad at you."

"Oh my God." Her eyes widened as she delivered another stinging slap to his bare chest. "You're horrible for letting me think—"

Clay crushed her mouth beneath his to shut her up.

He'd already been through the humiliation of having this woman fall asleep on him while he was pleasuring her. He wasn't about to sit quietly while she yelled at him now. Besides, they were in the middle of something he'd like to finish.

She continued to try to talk through the kiss. He

tilted his head and added his tongue, filling her mouth, then slid one hand between them and found her clit, adding the pressure of his finger while he pressed his length deep inside her.

Finally, she stopped talking.

It seemed he'd found a pretty good solution to keep her from arguing with him. Something they could both enjoy.

The only sound from Tasha now was a small moan of pleasure from deep in her throat. It produced an image of what else he would enjoy deep in her throat as he silenced her bitching with his cock in her mouth.

Oh yeah. There it was. That tingle he got from knowing that even with as much as she disliked him sometimes and wanted to fight, she still couldn't resist him.

It was like a testosterone and adrenaline cocktail shot straight into his bloodstream.

He thrust harder as he tried to ignore the knowledge that there was no doubt in his mind now that—bad idea or not—they were definitely going to do this again.

Tonight. Tomorrow. The night after that . . .

CHAPTER TWENTY-SIX

The problem with really good sex was that once Tasha had it, she wanted to have it again. And even though she could still feel the twinge of soreness from last night, she was more than ready for more tonight.

Frustrated, she glanced at the time on her cell phone. Nearly eleven. That she was still awake at that hour wasn't as frustrating as the fact she had full signal bars on her cell.

That meant one thing—Clay hadn't performed whatever magic he did that turned off the cameras, which meant she wasn't going to get what she wanted tonight.

To hell with that. She was a modern woman. She could ask for what she wanted.

Tasha typed in a text.

My cell phone is still working.

She sent it, hoping he'd pick up on her clever hint.

His reply came back fast.

I can see that.

Hmm. That wasn't what she wanted to see. Clay

was going to need another nudge apparently. He wasn't making this easy.

Can you make it stop working again?

There was a long pause after she hit send where there weren't even any of the telltale bubbles that told her he was typing a reply.

Finally, a text came through.

Give me a minute.

She smiled. Victory!

He hadn't even fought with her. Not today on camera. Not tonight when she'd not so subtly hinted she wanted a repeat of last night.

It had to be the sex. Two people—even two people who couldn't be more different and didn't agree on anything—couldn't be intimate and not get closer.

Her door swung open and Clay barreled in like a freight train. He didn't stop until he was hauling her off the bed by one arm and she was standing next to the bed.

He yanked her shorts down her legs, straightened and tugged her tank top over her head.

Fisting her hair he crushed his mouth against hers, plunging his tongue between her lips.

Caveman to the bone.

If he didn't stray from what she suspected was his usual sexual routine, she'd be on her back on the bed with him on top of her in seconds. She wasn't complaining. He was generous in the orgasm department, but for once it would be nice to feel as if she had some control over what happened between them.

He might be bigger, but she bet she could regain control.

Reaching between them, she slipped her hand into his shorts. The tip of his arousal was right there, barely contained below the waistband. He hissed in a breath through his nose as she delivered a stroke up and down the steely length.

She broke the kiss and turned, pushing him back onto the mattress like he usually did to her.

His lips quirked up in a smile. "What are you doing?"

"Taking control."

Clay's eyebrow rose. "Oh really. And what are you planning on doing with it after you take it?"

She hadn't thought that far ahead, but that was fine. She was good at improvising. "You'll see."

"All right." He leaned back on his elbows and waited, watching her.

This was clearly a case of be careful what you wished for because beneath his scrutiny as he waited with expectation she suddenly felt shy.

She had control of the situation, but what was she going to do with it?

There was one thing she always regretted. That while Clay was on top of her, she could never get a really good look at him.

At least not at all of him while he was naked. She wanted to study his tattoos. Run her hand and mouth over his muscles. Take her time and enjoy the man with a body the likes of which she'd only ever seen online or in the movies. Never up close and in person, never mind being able to touch and taste.

Pulling his T-shirt over his head, she tossed it onto the floor with hers and then moved in for the shorts. She was naked. It was only fair he should be too.

Once he was, she reached for the wall switch. The

overhead lights blared to life, making Clay frown. He looked at her questioningly.

"I want to see."

He let out a short laugh. "Okay."

Starting at his feet, she moved up his legs, running her fingers over the fine hairs. She stopped at a tattoo on his leg.

Leaning on one elbow she traced it with a fingertip. "What's this?"

"What's what?" he asked.

"This tattoo of frog bones."

"It's exactly that. Frog bones."

She frowned. "You're weird."

"And you're too close to my cock to not do something about it." He glanced at his hard length, bouncing against his stomach, and then pointedly back at her mouth, before he raised his gaze to her eyes.

She'd had every intention of doing what he'd hinted at even before he'd not so delicately suggested it. But that didn't mean she wasn't going to torture him first. "I haven't finished looking at all your many tattoos yet."

Tasha glanced down and ran her fingers over the U.S. Navy one with the anchor on his forearm before she moved up to the one of a cross with a name and date.

"They'll still be there later." He reached out and laid his big hand on the back of her head, nudging her gently downward.

There was still the tattoo of a pin-up girl sitting inside a martini glass she had yet to inspect, but obviously that would have to wait.

Somehow he was still in control, in spite of her

efforts. But there was one sure way she knew to bring a man to his knees. She leaned low and teased him with her tongue.

She tasted his tip before she slid her mouth down over his length.

He drew in a shaky breath and blew it out on a soft curse as he dropped his hand away from her. It landed on the mattress where he fisted a handful of the sheet.

She reached down and palmed his balls with one hand while stroking him with her other hand and mouth. He threw his head back against her pillow and let out a groan.

Who was in control now? As she felt his stomach heave and his legs tremble she knew the answer to that question. It might not last for long but for right now, it was all her.

CHAPTER TWENTY-SEVEN

When the cell vibrated at dawn on Clay's bedside table he pried open one tired eyelid.

What the hell? Tasha couldn't be booty-texting him again. He'd just left her bed a few hours ago. He hadn't even logged in five hours sleep yet.

He reached for the cell to shut this shit down. Sex was great, but a man needed some sleep sometimes. Especially a man forced to renovate a house on a crazy timeline while on camera.

The name on the display had him sighing. Only a SEAL would think texting at zero-five-hundred was okay. And normally it would have been.

A month ago, Clay would have been out for a run or at least up having coffee by sunrise. But nothing in his life was normal right now.

Hoping nothing was wrong, he opened the text and read it.

How's that jammer working out for you?

Clay could hear the laughter behind the words of Asher's text . . . and he didn't like it. He tapped in a reply.

Don't know. Haven't used it.

The response came fast and in all caps.

BULL SHIT YOU DIDN'T!!!

It was too early for this shit. Clay flopped back against his pillow and flung his forearm across his eyes. The phone still in his hand vibrated with a call.

With a sigh, Clay opened his eyes and swiped to connect. "Yeah?"

"No details for your old teammate? Come on, Dirtman. I deserve something."

"Oh, really. And why do you deserve something?"

"Because I'm wheels-up in an hour. You know this life, man. There's no guarantee I'll be back."

Clay widened his eyes. "You sick mother fucker. You did not just say that to me."

"Why not? It's true."

Playing the death card just days after Randy's annual memorial was low. Fucking Asher knew exactly how to play him and dammit it was working.

He groaned. "Fine. Yes, dickhead. I used it."

"Oh my God. Do tell. I want details."

"Well, you can't have them." Clay glanced at the camera in the corner of his room. It was back up and running and recording audio along with video, so there'd be no spilling of secrets here and now—not that he'd have given Asher any details at any time.

"Come on," Asher prodded.

Letting out a huge breath of frustration, Clay flung back the covers and planted his two bare feet on the bare wood floors. He might as well get up. He was awake now.

Asher continued, "You can't hide her away now that I've met her. She's even cuter in person than online."

"So? This is California. Cute girls are everywhere." Clay made his way to the bathroom. The one place he could speak in moderate privacy. Besides, he had to take a piss.

"And yet you never moved in to live with any of them. In fact, you've managed to not have a serious, long term girlfriend for all the many years I've known you."

"We're not living together. It's just for the show," he hissed it low as he cradled the cell on his shoulder and aimed for the bowl. "And as for a relationship, you know the life we live. There was no room for serious relationships."

"Ah, but see, there's one problem with that. You're no longer in the teams. You're out of excuses, my friend."

Clay scowled. He didn't need the reminder. Retirement had been the biggest change of his life. But as for the other thing Asher had said, that he was out of excuses, that was bullshit. He hadn't even come close to exhausting his reasons as to why he and Tasha would never work.

He knew the list by heart. In the bedroom, they might mesh for an hour at a time. But the rest of the time, and in the running pros versus cons list in his head, the two of them just didn't work.

It was simple. This relationship was fueled by sex. Once he was away from whatever pheromones she was emitting like some sort of frigging siren's call he'd be fine.

Unfortunately, now that Asher had grabbed on to the subject, he wasn't likely to let it go. He'd go on teasing Clay long after they'd wrapped up this production and he and Tasha had both moved on with their lives.

Clay ignored the pressure in his chest at the thought that day was rapidly approaching and said, "What are you bored? Why are you so interested in my life? They not keeping you busy there?"

"Don't change the subject," Asher replied.

"Then don't be an ass," Clay countered, trying to figure out how to get his friend off the subject of Tasha—or at least off the phone.

Before he figured that out, Asher said, "Shit. Gotta go."

Clay knew what that meant. There was no more joking between them as he said, "Okay. Be safe. Love ya', brother."

"Right back at ya'. And I expect you'll have something to report by the time I get back."

Clay just shook his head. They didn't have the time to argue more on this subject. "See you on the flip side."

"You got it." The call went dead as Asher disconnected, leaving Clay standing in the bathroom with his cell in hand.

He fought a turmoil of emotions, torn between disappointment that he was now an outsider after being on the inside for twenty years, and relief that while the team was kitting up to fly God only knew where, the only thing he had to do today was drive to Home Depot and work on his beach house.

And once the house was done, then what?

Running on the beach, catching a few waves, sipping a cold brew while grilling a burger—it had all seemed like retirement paradise. But was it going to be enough?

He was barely forty. God willing he had another

forty good years left. Were his short term plans going to satisfy him for the long haul?

Clay had a feeling he knew the answer, but he didn't like it.

He glanced at the time on his cell. It was too late to go back to sleep and too early to start work, but it was a perfect time for a sunrise run on the beach.

Hopefully it would clear his head.

Who knew? Maybe he'd have some sort of endorphin-induced epiphany about what to do with the rest of his life. Stranger things had happened.

CHAPTER TWENTY-EIGHT

"Where's Clay?" Maria asked as she plopped down in a folding chair and her assistant scurried to set the to-go coffee cup in front of her.

Tasha took a sip of hot coffee from her own ceramic mug. She'd decided to make herself at home, even if it were for only a short time, so she'd grabbed her coffee maker and her favorite mug when she'd snuck to her condo the other day.

She'd brewed a pot this morning and had noticed the aroma hadn't lured Clay out of his room. He wasn't one to sleep in, so she'd gotten worried and checked his room. The bed was made and he was nowhere to be found. But his running shoes were missing from where they lived just inside the back door.

"I'm not certain, but I think he's out for a run," Tasha answered. She glanced at the time on her cell. "It's still early. Hopefully, he's back soon."

Maria nodded. "I guess staying in that kind of shape takes work." She grinned at Tasha, who really couldn't argue since she'd been up close and personal with Clay's amazingly hard body just hours ago.

She made a non-committal sound of agreement and took another sip of coffee, hoping the evidence that she'd just been picturing Clay naked in her bed wasn't showing on her face.

"So I had editing put together a promo trailer."

Tasha nodded. "The one that's on the show's social media pages."

"No, actually, a new one. I sent it to the network and they've been airing it on cable."

They had no cable hookup—and no television—in the house, not that she'd have had time to watch between the renovations and sex with Clay anyway.

She cleared her throat and dragged her mind off that. "Really. Wow. I'd love to see it."

"I'll email you a link to the file. It's being received really well. Even better than Joanne had hoped and trust me she had some high expectations."

A smiling director and a happy executive producer was a very good thing. Tasha decided to take advantage of it. "Since the show's getting a lot of good buzz already, have you started thinking about season two?"

"We can't invest in another property until we see some ratings and get a commitment from the network so we know there will be a season two, but yeah, we've been talking about it at the head office."

"Oh? Any plans you can share?" Tasha asked.

Maria drew in a breath. "I'll be perfectly honest with you. They're planning on playing up the couple aspect again, since it's proving so popular, so with a new project there will also be a new team of co-hosts for the second season."

Feeling a little sick to her stomach, she said, "But

Clay and I aren't a couple."

Tasha tried to read the meaning behind Maria's shrug. Did it mean Maria didn't believe her denial, or that it didn't matter either way because Clay had made it clear this season was a one shot deal?

That gave Tasha an idea. "What if I got Clay to agree to do another season? With me, on a new project."

"Do you think you could convince him to do that?" Maria asked.

"Possibly. I mean he's retired now from the Navy. What else does he have to do?"

Why wouldn't he want to do it? He'd get paid. And he have the time once this house was finished. She might have to get creative in the bedroom to make him see the light, but that could be fun . . . for both of them.

Tasha glanced up to see Maria nodding.

"That's right. He is a veteran, isn't he? We should probably play up that aspect more." Maria scribbled something in her notebook before, finally, she looked back to Tasha. "All right. I'll present the idea to Joanne and see what her thoughts are on it. In the meantime, you feel out Clay and see if he's onboard."

"See if I'm onboard for what?" Clay's booming voice brought Tasha's attention around to where his bulk filled the back door that he'd apparently slipped through while she'd been occupied with the conversation.

She needed time to ease him into the idea, so Tasha scrambled to come up with something to say besides the truth. "For shopping for the furniture for the house together on camera."

She saw Maria smirk at her outright lie before she

glanced back to Clay, who was frowning.

With a scowl, he said, "I'm taking a shower."

"But what do you think about my idea?" she called after him as he walked away. She really did want to take the cameras to a furniture store before the end of production.

Without turning around, he said, "I'll think about it."

That was better than a *no*. Satisfied, Tasha leaned back in her chair and reached for her mug.

Maria let out a laugh. "I'm starting to think you might actually be able to convince him to do another season."

Tasha hoped so. Her career could depend on it . . . and after the past couple of nights they'd spent together, the idea of keeping Clay close for another season   definitely   had   its   appeal.

CHAPTER TWENTY-NINE

Reclining in Tasha's bed for the third night in a row, Clay watched her trace the outline of the cross on his arm with one fingertip. It was the tattoo he'd gotten the day after Randy's funeral. "You're so enthralled with my tattoos, why don't you get one of your own?"

She shrugged and glanced up. "I guess I don't feel like I've got something important enough to immortalize, like you do."

Her gaze dropped to the name and date before she drew in a breath and slid down his body. He never objected to her moving her mouth closer to his cock, but that wasn't where she was aiming. Instead she was heading down the bed to take a closer look at his bone frog.

"They don't all have to represent something important. This one was just something I liked." He pointed to the Sailor Jerry design on his chest—a girl in a martini glass.

Although that one actually did have a deeper meaning too, he supposed. The guys on the team called him Dirty Martini—shortened to Dirtman most of the time—because that's what he ordered when he was in the mood to really drink.

"The frog one's got numbers underneath it. What do they mean?" Tasha was back on the subject of the one tattoo he wished she'd ignore.

He'd avoided telling her the real meaning of the tat before. Tonight, avoidance seemed too close to lying and, like it or not, after spending three nights in a row in her bed—and inside her—he couldn't lie.

"That's the number of my BUD/S class."

Her head whipped up. "Your what?"

"Every Navy SEAL class is given a number."

It was a vain hope that he'd be able to distract her with facts. It was clear she was less interested in military trivia and more concerned with why he'd never disclosed what he'd really done while in the military.

"What? You never told me you were a SEAL."

"You never asked."

"And Randy? And Asher? Them too?"

He tipped his head.

Tasha blew out a breath. "I guess I should have guessed. I mean McP's is full of SEAL stuff."

"You mad?" he asked, surprised that she didn't seem pissed. And just as surprised she didn't kick him out of her bed while screeching at him.

She lifted a shoulder. "No. Not really. I know how you are."

Clay lifted a brow. "And how am I?"

Tasha laughed. "So many words come to mind, but if I were to choose just one, I'd go with uncommunicative."

He bobbed his head. Her word could have been

worse. "I can live with that."

Reaching down he grabbed her by both shoulders and pulled her up to him.

She bit her bottom lip and her eyes locked on his. "Any other secrets I should know about? Wives? Kids? Felonies?"

He smiled. "No to all of the above."

"Okay. I can live with that." She moved in and then she was biting his lip instead of her own and he could definitely live with that.

A few days later, Clay realized they'd fallen into a pattern.

For almost a week now he'd done the same thing. Jam the signal. Have sex. Sneak out of Tasha's room before dawn to turn off the jammer and slide into bed for a few hours sleep before the crew arrived.

He'd gotten more sleep when he'd been a SEAL, but he wasn't going to complain. This was a short-term deal anyway.

In spite of his doubts about the timeline, the project was progressing and basically on schedule. Soon the house would be done. The show would be over and he'd have his peaceful sanctuary back after Tasha moved back to her own place.

That would be the perfect time to break off this new habit of theirs.

So why did he wonder if she'd text him from her bed after she'd moved out? And, dammit, he knew if she did he'd be over there or she'd be over here half an hour later.

What exactly did that make them? Friends with benefits maybe? Though they weren't exactly friends. More like coworkers.

Fuck buddies? That didn't exactly fit the bill either.

They'd actually started to talk in between rounds of sex. Not fight. Not sex talk. But actual conversations.

He didn't want to think the other word to describe what they might be because they were *not* a couple.

They'd never been on a date. They didn't hold hands or call each other *baby*. This wasn't a relationship. It was sex. Nothing more.

As he flopped over on his bed, trying and failing to get comfortable, the cross on his arm caught his eye. He remembered Tasha's gentle touch as she ran her fingers over it. Remembered the genuine concern in her eyes when he'd told her at McP's about Randy's death.

He wasn't such a course Neanderthal as she made him out to be. Like it or not, he had feelings and this thing between them was starting to feel like more than just sex— He didn't want that.

Not with a woman who lived in a different world than he did. She thrived in the bright lights of the camera while he sought the shadows, just as he had for years as a SEAL.

The man who ended up with Tasha Jones might always live in her shadow, but it would be a shadow cast by a spotlight.

That woman would die if her life weren't on display in the most public manner. The thought of that made his skin crawl. He was comfortable being invisible.

Why was he even thinking about her or them together? She'd made no secret from the beginning that she thought he was beneath her. A woman like that would never be happy with a man like him for more than the couple of hours a night while he pleased her in bed.

In fact, he should probably feel used. He might, if he wasn't enjoying their time together just as much as she was.

Yup. He'd be sorry when it ended, but he'd never admit that to her—or Asher or any of the other guys.

It was enough he'd finally admitted it to himself. That was progress in his personal growth.

The sky was growing brighter outside his window and it was pretty clear he wasn't going to get any more sleep this morning. He sat up and decided to see what was going on in the world since he'd been living in a bubble of renovations and sex for the past couple of weeks.

He hadn't gotten around to hooking up the television he stashed in the garage, so he grabbed his cell phone and opened the cable company's app.

There, he navigated through the channel lineup.

He might be a caveman, as Tasha called him, but he wasn't ignorant when it came to technology. He'd long ago learned how to find a way to stream onto his phone. All he needed was some kind of a signal and somebody's log in information—usually his parents'—and he'd manage it.

Sometimes it was glitchy, yeah. Sometimes it required jumping through hoops or dancing along the line of being illegal, but he'd found a way to watch at least something in most places in the world.

Here, it was easy. They had kick ass, high-speed Wi-Fi set up in the house and were close enough to the city he could log in to see all the cable channels he could ever want plus the local stations.

As he scrolled through the channel guide on the cell, he paused when he saw an ad pop up between the listings.

It caught his eye because it was his own fucking eyes he saw. It was a picture of him in uniform. It was his last official military photo taken before he'd retired.

He hit the ad and it sent him to a webpage for the show. He read the headline.

One Navy SEAL. One television star. What happens when they're thrown together into the renovation zone? You get one Hot House! Coming soon, only on THN—The Home Nation station.

There was a video on the page. He hit the screen to play it. It was a montage of scenes and—*mother fucker*—one of them had just been filmed two days ago. He recognized the shirt Tasha had been wearing.

This video was brand new. It had obviously been put together in the last couple of days—*after* he'd told Tasha he was a SEAL.

They showed his official military photo again, zooming in on the medals on his chest before it cut to a shot that stoked his rage to the danger zone. It was the framed photo that he knew was hanging on the wall behind the bar of McP's. It was of him and the team.

His head nearly exploded when he recognized it. It had been taken on the first anniversary of Randy's death. They all sat around the table, drinks raised while Randy's shot sat on the table in front of an empty chair.

How the fuck did they even know to go to McP's if Tasha hadn't told them?

Exploiting him was one thing. But to bring the other guys into this—to capitalize on the death his friend—it was inexcusable.

He'd confided in Tasha and she'd run right to the

producers and told them everything. She was so desperate to be a star she didn't care who she bowled over to do it.

Of course the producers would jump right on this information. Him being a SEAL was something they could use.

Jaw set, he didn't care he was only wearing underwear, he stood and strode across his bedroom. He flung open his bedroom door so hard it crashed against the wall. He crossed the hall to Tasha's door.

He didn't knock. He just stormed into her room. "What the fuck is this?"

Looking half asleep, she struggled to sit up in bed. "What's what? What's wrong?"

"This video." He held up his cell phone as proof even though she couldn't see it from where she was. "You told them I was a SEAL?"

"No." She shook her head. "I haven't told anybody."

"Don't bother lying. Somebody told and you're the only one who knew."

"Clay, I didn't tell anyone."

"Then how do they know?" he accused.

"Maybe your little signal jammer doesn't jam as well as you think it does and they heard. You ever think of that?"

His gaze shot to the camera in the corner of the room. "Thanks. Now they know about that too."

Her eyes widened. "I thought you would have turned it on before you came in."

"I didn't." Though he should have.

She had him so crazed. Christ, what was happening to him? He used to be able to take on any situation, face all adversity, with the calm of a monk.

Thank God he wasn't in the teams anymore. The way he was now, he would have gotten them all killed.

He'd lost his edge. Lost his cool.

Hell, he'd lost his damn mind and it was all her fault.

"Doesn't matter anyway. I won't be using the jammer again. Believe me."

She breathed faster as her eyes narrowed. She'd read the meaning behind his words, as he'd intended her to. There'd be no more midnight booty calls. No more pillow talk and sharing secrets.

They were done.

Maria and Joanne and the rest of them would be lucky if he could bring himself to speak civilly to her for the last week of production.

They'd taken advantage of his service to his nation without his permission. It would serve them right if he didn't speak to Tasha again and ruined the show.

"Fine," she spat. "You don't believe me, but it doesn't matter anyway. We're almost done with the show. I'll tell Joanne we're doing the press tour separately so we won't have to see each other."

"Press?" He let out a bitter laugh. "I might have sold my soul for this house but I didn't agree to any press tour."

"Oh no? Maybe you should have gotten someone a little smarter than you to read over your contract, sweetie, because you certainly did agree to promotion."

He dragged in an angry breath as she called him stupid to his face. She was a conceited, superior diva who always had and always would look down on him, just as he'd thought.

His heart raced and his pulse pounded, but his

brain somehow managed to still function. Or maybe it was pure gut instinct, but he knew if he didn't get out of there he was going to do or say something he might regret later—and the camera was going to record it all.

Turning, he left her and everything they'd shared together behind him.

CHAPTER THIRTY

Tasha drew in a shaky stuttering breath as her tears turned into sobs.

Pacing her bedroom like a caged animal, she pressed the cell closer to her ear. "He's such an ass. I thought we were getting a—along. But he hates me more than ever. Call me when you wake up. Please."

She disconnected the call. Her rant was only on Jane's voicemail, but it helped to get it out to somebody.

Clay was an ass, just as she'd thought he was in the beginning, before she'd let sex cloud her better judgment.

He was insane. Off the rails. Accusing her of doing all sorts of things she hadn't done.

What proof did he have to come in her room at the crack of dawn all scary like that?

He had Navy and SEAL tattoos all over him, so why did he assume it was her who told? Lots of people had to know he was a SEAL. It wasn't like those things were kept secret. Were they?

And she still didn't know what video he was

talking about when he waved his cell phone at her.

Calming enough to think, she remembered Maria had mentioned a promo spot the network had been running. She'd said she'd email the link to Tasha, but she hadn't checked her inbox in days.

Her days here were so messed up she had no set routine and things that used to be built into her morning schedule, such as checking her email, had fallen by the wayside.

What the hell had been in that video that had set him off? It had to have been bad. She grabbed her laptop, leaning against the wall where she had it plugged in and charging. She could check for Maria's email right now and solve this mystery. Then she'd go and confront Clay and make him apologize.

She had to scroll past lots of junk in her inbox, but finally she found an email from Maria from three days ago. She hit the link that took her to a video promo spot.

Clay was smiling in one shot, and frowning at her in the next as she held up a paint sample he hadn't liked.

She saw herself, eyeing Clay as if she were picturing him naked as he bent over to pick up a hammer. Actually, she remembered that day and she had been imagining just that. She saw herself again tripping over a broom and careening into a table where an open gallon of paint sat, before Clay caught her and prevented both her and the paint can from toppling over.

There was nothing about him being a SEAL. In fact, there was nothing bad at all that should have angered him.

If anything she should be the one upset. In less

than a minute of footage they'd made her look like a bumbling buffoon while Clay looked like the hero.

So what was his problem?

She wiped her eyes and set down the laptop. She wanted to make herself a cup of coffee—maybe the caffeine would help her think—but she was afraid he was out there.

Hurt and mad, she wasn't sure she wanted to see him right now.

The sound of his truck starting in the driveway sent her running to the window. His room faced the ocean, but her room faced the street and today that provided exactly the view she needed of Clay peeling backwards out of the driveway before he took off down the road.

She shook her head. Driving like that, he was going to get himself or someone else killed. She was mad and upset, but not enough to wish him dead.

Great. Now she was going to have to worry about him until he got back—*if* he came back.

What if he quit? What would happen to the show? What would happen to his house? Would Joanne hold him in breach of contract? They could take the house. That was spelled out clearly in the papers he'd signed.

He wouldn't walk away. He might hate her, but he loved this house and he wouldn't risk it.

Tasha blew out a breath—mad at herself for being concerned about a man who obviously didn't give a crap about her.

It might not be safe on the roadways with Clay out there and in a bad mood, but at least it was safe for her to go to the kitchen.

She washed her face, brushed her teeth and threw on shorts and a T-shirt for the day before she made her way out to the kitchen.

After starting the coffee, she was waiting as the glass carafe slowly filled when the front door swung open.

Heart racing, she leaned out of the kitchen and peeked at the front door, but it wasn't Clay. It was Greg, the cameraman.

"Hey." He moved into the kitchen and glanced around. "Where's the big guy?"

"Gone."

"Gone where?"

"Your guess is as good as mine. He had a meltdown about the video promo and stormed out."

"The newest one that just started airing today?"

"Wait, today? I didn't know there was another one. I thought he was upset about the one that's been airing on the network all week. Maria told me about it days ago."

He shook his head. "No. There's a brand new cut. The ads went live at midnight."

It was starting to make more sense now. God, what was in this new one? Whatever it was had pushed him over the edge. With a sense of dread, she asked, "What's in it?"

Greg pulled his cell out of his pocket and poked at the screen before thrusting it toward Tasha. "Here. See for yourself."

She pushed to play the video and saw Clay in his Navy dress uniform looking devastatingly handsome.

Nothing about that should have freaked him out, but then the shot cut to a photo. From among those in the group of men she recognized Clay and his friend Asher, the guy she'd met at McP's.

Again, she couldn't understand what was so bad

about that. Sure, he was a private person and she knew he didn't want his friends on camera, which is why he'd snuck out and ditched his cameraman when he went out to meet them, but it wasn't anything to be so angry about.

The voice over and text was pretty generic. It basically portrayed Clay as a guy's guy and her as a girly girl.

It showed how opposite they were and posed the question of what would happen when these two unlikely people were thrown into the renovation zone together for twenty-four hours a day.

The video ended and she handed the cell back. "I guess he was mad because he thought I told Maria that he'd been a SEAL. For some reason he didn't want anyone to know, but I didn't tell her."

"I know you didn't." Greg nodded. "I did."

"You? How did you know? I didn't know until he finally told me the other night—um, you know, after you guys left but before I went to bed. In my room."

Shit. She was bad at lying.

He let out a short laugh. "How could you not know? Didn't you see his bone frog tattoo? That's a SEAL thing."

She scowled. "I'm sorry but frog bones don't exactly scream Navy SEAL to me."

Jeez. He was acting like it was common knowledge and she was the only one in the world who didn't know it.

"Well, it is a Navy SEAL thing so when Maria was talking about wanting to play up Clay's time in the Navy in some promo I said how cool it would be to mention the fact the SEALs train in Coronado, which isn't that far from here." Greg continued, "Maria seemed so interested that I told her she should check out the bars in Coronado where the SEALs hang out because they have some cool memorabilia on the walls. Lots of history. So she and I went over together to shoot some B-roll."

"McP's," Tasha said under her breath. She glanced up. "McP's Pub is where Maria and Joanne first met Clay."

He nodded. "Yup. That's what she said so she and I went there and boy did we strike pay dirt. That's where we found the picture of Clay and his teammates."

Tasha's brain spun with a detail that had escaped her before. "Can I see that video again?" she asked.

"Sure." He unlocked the cell and handed it to her.

She watched the video again, pausing it on the shot of the photo.

Zooming in she looked closer and blew out a breath. Not one of the men seated at that table was smiling like you'd expect from a group of guys out at a bar.

Clay had told her they all got together annually in honor of their fallen teammate.

There was something written in the corner of the photo that she couldn't read. What if it said RIP? Or his friend's name and the date he'd died, just like Clay's tattoo did?

This photo was very likely meant to be a memorandum to the SEAL who had died . . . and Clay thought she'd taken the information he'd shared with her and no one else and that she'd passed it on to the producers to be used to promote the show.

No wonder he was mad at her. He had every right to be angry. But it hadn't been her and she needed him to know that.

It might be over, whatever it had been between them, but she couldn't stand having him think she'd do something like that.

"Greg, would you tell Clay what you just told me? Let him know it wasn't me who told Maria. Please?"

He nodded. "Yeah, sure. I honestly didn't think it would be a problem."

"I know. I think it's more that he thinks I took something he told me in confidence and went behind his back to Maria with it to promote the show. It's the betrayal, more than it getting out that he'd been a SEAL. You understand?"

He nodded. "Gotcha. Wouldn't want to get between the two love birds."

"What? Wait. We're not lovebirds," she sputtered.

He smiled. "Whatever. Don't worry, Tash. I'll let him know it wasn't you who told Maria."

"Thanks." She blew out a breath, not happy with his smirk, but she could live with it as long as he straightened things out with Clay.

"I'm gonna go get the rest of the equipment out of the van." Greg tipped his head toward the front door.

"Okay." Happy he'd left again so she could be alone to absorb everything she'd learned in the past few minutes, Tasha moved to the cabinet and reached for her mug on the nearly empty shelf.

Looking at the bare cupboard, she couldn't help but feel sorry for Clay. Except for his SEAL buddies, which she wasn't sure he saw all that much anymore, he really was a loner. And he thought the one person he'd opened up to had betrayed him. She needed to fix this.

Her phone rang and she glanced down, half

hoping to see Clay's name. Instead she saw Jane's.

"Hello," she answered.

"Tasha, sweetie. I can barely understand your message. I'm still half asleep and I haven't had my coffee yet, so you're going to have to calm down and tell me again what happened."

"Oh, Jane. Things are so messed up."

"Talk to me."

Cradling her cell against her shoulder, Tasha poured herself a mug of coffee and carried it back to her bedroom. She needed a good gab session and Jane was just the girl for it.

CHAPTER THIRTY-ONE

Clay wrapped his hands around the steaming hot mug of coffee as his cell phone vibrated for the fifth time in a row with an incoming text.

The bartender glanced down at it and then back up at Clay. "You gonna check that?"

"Nope."

"All right." Raymond dumped ice into the bin and carried the empty bucket back to the kitchen, leaving Clay momentarily alone in the bar.

He returned shortly with a rack full of glasses and Clay watched as he took each one out, wiped it with a white towel and put it on the shelf.

"Thanks for letting me in early. And for the coffee."

"Sure." Ray shrugged. "I don't mind the company. And you looked like you needed a place to hide."

The cell on the bar vibrated one more time, proving Ray was correct. Clay was hiding and apparently they were looking for him.

He should have been back at the house over an hour ago. He'd deliberately stayed away and obviously he'd been missed.

Not that he knew for sure who was texting or what they were saying since his cell was facedown on the bar and he'd refused to let himself look. He didn't need any more of Tasha's lies.

"So who are you avoiding?" Ray asked.

Clay laughed. "Everyone. Except you, that is."

"I'm honored." Ray rolled his eyes as the cell vibrated a sixth time. "Why don't you just turn it off?"

"I guess I like knowing they're freaking out."

Ray's raised eyebrows told Clay his opinion on the matter.

With a sigh, Clay picked up the cell and looked at the many message alerts. His cameraman. Maria. Tasha.

Yup. Pretty much who he expected to see. The whole cast of characters.

He blew out a breath and started with the first one, Greg asking where he was. That was followed by Tasha saying she knew he was angry but she could explain. A second one from her asked him to please come back to the house because Maria was really pissed.

Next was Maria, threatening to sue him if he didn't get his ass to the house immediately. The next one was Greg saying he had something important to tell him, man to man, privately. That was followed by another one swearing it wasn't a trick to get him to set and it had nothing to do with Maria.

That last one was interesting.

Clay supposed it didn't hurt to find out more. It was probably time to head back, but only because he was curious what the cameraman had to say. That was all. His interest had nothing to do with the fact that Tasha had betrayed him and that something in him wanted someone to provide a reason, an excuse, why she'd done it.

Usually fighting with Tasha made him want to grab her hair in his fist and bury his cock deep inside her. But this, this wasn't like that. Somehow this—hurt.

He didn't like that she had the power to make him feel like this. The power to drive him from his own damn house.

She didn't. No one did. He'd left before he'd lost what little control he'd had left and done something destructive. That was all. And now he was choosing to go back.

He pushed the coffee mug away from him and climbed off the barstool. Digging his wallet out of his pocket he said, "What do I owe you?"

Raymond waved off the offer. "On the house."

Clay tossed a couple of dollars on the bar for a tip and nodded. "Thanks. And not just for coffee."

Someplace to lay low and think was what he'd really needed, more than the caffeine. Ray had provided that and he was grateful.

"Anytime, Dirtman. But can I offer you some advice?"

Clay paused half turned toward the exit and glanced back. "I guess that's part of your job as bartender so sure. Why not?"

"Whatever happened that had you waiting for me to get here this morning, whoever he or she is, deal with it. You gotta face it, man. Head on. Don't wait too long. That shit just festers if you let it go on too long."

Clay knew Raymond was right, but he didn't want to admit it and he really didn't want to face Tasha again just yet.

It was ridiculous. He'd run full steam ahead and faced some of the world's worst men without hesitation, yet one woman half his body weight had driven him into hiding.

Though not just Tasha. Maria and Joanne and New Millennia Media had done their part as well. He had enough anger to spread around.

Clay tipped his head to acknowledge he'd heard Ray's advice. Whether he'd heed it and let Tasha explain her actions or not was yet to be determined, but he was done avoiding his own home.

He got to his truck and texted back Greg, telling him he was on his way to talk to him and him alone, no one else, and if they knew what was good for them everyone else would stay away.

As an afterthought he sent a second text, smiling with an inner evil.

Remember I'm a SEAL. We're trained to kill with our bare hands.

That should do it. If they wanted to use his years in the service to their advantage, then he could damn well use it to his own.

Less than fifteen minutes later, Clay pulled up to the curb. He'd calmed down during the drive but the sight of his driveway sent his heart thundering again.

There was barely enough space in the driveway for Tasha's car, Maria's car, and one of the production vans parked there, forget about his truck. He was ready for this shit to be over.

Best to not block anyone in. With any luck, one or all of them would leave—and leave him the fuck alone.

Yeah, right. No such luck.

He noticed the HVAC van parked across the street. Today they were putting in a new heat and A/C unit. One more thing that could get checked off the to-do list—one step closer to his being able to close this nightmare chapter of his life.

Speaking of nightmares . . . Tasha came out of the house and walked up to his truck.

He cursed to himself, drew in a breath and opened the door. Before she had a chance to say anything to piss him off, he said, "I told Greg I'd talk to him alone and that everybody else needed to stay the fuck out of my way today."

She opened her mouth to speak and he held up his hand to stop her.

"I know. I know there's a fucking contract. I know I'm obligated to finish this fucking show or get sued, but not today. I'm too pissed off to play house with you for the cameras. Film something else. I'll start back tomorrow."

"Maria already rearranged the schedule to do exactly that. That's why Greg isn't here. She sent him to get some shots of the town and the beach for B-roll."

"Then why didn't he text me and tell me that?" Clay pulled out his cell and blew out a breath when he saw the unread text from Greg that must have come in while he was driving.

He punched the screen to open it and just as Tasha had said, Greg said he'd gotten pulled away. But he also said something else. He said to hear Tasha out and believe what she said. That it wasn't her. It had been him.

There wasn't enough information in the text. It forced him to do the one thing he didn't want to do—talk to Tasha and trust her to tell him the truth.

Clay glanced up, angry, tired—tired of being angry. "I don't understand what he's saying. What does he mean it wasn't you, it was him?"

"Greg recognized your frog tattoo. I heard he used to be embedded with a combat reporter so he knows military stuff. He's the one who told Maria you were a SEAL, not me. She took him to McP's to get some shots of all the SEAL memorabilia hanging on the walls. She remembered all that stuff was there from when we had our first meeting. Remember?"

He'd never forget. That was the day this hell began. Scowling, he nodded.

"Anyway, it was a complete coincidence that while they were taking close-ups of some of the things, they found that picture of you." She hesitated. "I watched the video and saw the picture. You guys were there for Randy, weren't you?"

His nostrils flared, hating that Randy's name was even on her lips. "Maria know that?" he asked.

Tasha shook her head emphatically. "No. I think she thought it was just a picture of you getting drunk with some buddies."

He shook his head, torn between thinking it was bull, and that it sounded just crazy enough to be plausible. At this point he didn't trust his own instincts.

"When you came into my room this morning . . ." She apparently wasn't done yet. "The only new video I knew about was from like four days ago. Maria had told me about it. I hadn't even seen that last one myself. I knew nothing about this latest one, I swear.

They never run these things by me. I have to find out by seeing them online or by asking Maria to send me a link, but I can only ask for that if I know they made a new one."

She was babbling, but the more she talked the more she deflated his case against her. It was even getting hard to be mad at Maria.

It seemed this was just a series of coincidences and dumb luck. That his cameraman recognized his bone frog. That Maria happened to see that picture at McP's. That she and Tasha had met there for their business that first day so she even knew the place existed. And that the one picture of him at McP's happened to be from the first year anniversary of Randy's death.

His eyes cut to where Tasha touched his arm. She withdrew her fingers immediately.

Smart girl. Just because he wasn't still pissed enough to kill someone didn't mean he was ready to make nice.

"Do you believe me?" she asked, her voice soft and unsure.

Did he? Yeah, he did. And that meant he'd been wrong to jump to conclusions and accuse her. Which also meant, technically, he owed her an apology.

Fuck. He hated apologizing. But he'd been wrong and there was no way around it.

"I'm sorry I—"

"No. Don't apologize. I understand." She laid her hand on his arm again. "If I'd only told one person a bunch of private things and then two days later a video appeared that had all of those things in it, I would make the same assumption."

He pressed his lips together. "Thanks for

understanding, but I was wrong and I need to apologize. I'm sorry."

"Thanks." She nodded, her eyes looking teary.

Damn women and their tears. They knew exactly how to make a man feel worse than he already did.

He let out a bitter laugh. "You know, in the beginning, I kind of enjoyed arguing with you."

She smiled while looking a bit sad. "I know. Me too."

"But this time." He shook his head. "I didn't like it."

"I didn't like it either." She raised her gaze to his. "What do you think that means?"

He ran his tongue over his teeth, considering, stalling, not wanting to accept what he thought it meant.

"What do you think it means?" he asked, turning the question back on her.

She broke eye contact, kicking her flip-flop against the driveway. For the first time he noticed she was dressed more like he usually was, than like herself. Shorts and a T-shirt rather than a dress and impractical heels. He'd rubbed off on her.

Finally, she said, "I think we might have become friends. Or more . . . maybe." She forced her gaze up. "What do you think?"

He thought that if he didn't get this woman somewhere private soon, he'd embarrass them both.

Whether it was the adrenaline from the anger and their fight or the relief she hadn't done what he'd thought . . . or maybe it was just the fact he was finally ready to admit his feelings and embrace the possibilities of a relationship, it was clear to him. They weren't fuck buddies. They weren't friends with

213

benefits. She'd said it first and he agreed, they were more.

More. Yeah, that's exactly how it felt. That was a perfect word for it.

He took a step forward and raised both hands to her arms. "I think you're right."

"You do?" she asked, her eyes widening.

He laughed. "Yes. Is that such a surprise?"

"You saying I'm right? Yes. Yes, it is a surprise."

"Well, this is different."

"How?" she asked.

"This isn't about my house, which is my domain. So, you know, I have to be right when it comes to that."

She laughed. "And now you're making jokes? And jokes about having to be right all the time?" Tasha narrowed her eyes and looked him up and down. "Where is the real Clay and what have you done with him? Is this some sort of alien abduction scenario?"

He smiled. "Nope. It's really me."

She took a step forward. Now they were standing so close they were nearly touching. "So what changed? What happened to you?"

"You happened to me," he admitted.

"I did?" She bit her lip and her eyes got glassy.

He cursed beneath his breath. "You know damn well, you did."

She bit her lip again and it was all he could do to not take the plump flesh between his own teeth.

In fact, the moment they were alone, he was going to do just that, before he moved down her body and nibbled on some other plump and fleshy lips he had a craving for.

"So what do we do now?" she asked.

214

Ah, the future. That was a topic he'd always avoided with females. Run from it like it was a grenade about to go off.

This time he wouldn't run, but that didn't mean he had an answer for her.

"Well, the next couple of weeks are set. We finish the house. We do whatever promotional bullshit Maria forces me to do."

She laughed, probably at his obvious hatred of publicity.

He lifted a shoulder. "After that . . . I honestly don't know. When I retired and then found this house I thought I'd be happy just sitting around enjoying doing nothing for the rest of my life. Now, I'm not so sure." He glanced down at her. "What about you?"

She pressed her lips together and avoided eye contact. When she finally looked at him she said, "I don't know. They said if the show gets picked up for another season they're going to look for new hosts."

"Why? Why couldn't you do it?"

"They don't want me without you."

"What? Why not?"

"Because they said the reason the show works is the, um, sexual tension between you and me. And they wouldn't want to keep me and replace you with another guy so they'd rather get a new couple for the next house project."

He frowned. "What if I stayed on? Would they agree to keeping you on, both of us, for the next project?"

She drew her head back. "You'd do that? Do another season even though you hated this one so much?"

"I didn't hate it—"

"Clay . . ."

"Okay, at times I hated it. But there were some parts I grew to like." He squeezed her arms. "More than liked."

Her expression softened. "I more than liked certain parts too."

He smiled. "So we tell Maria we're a team and they take us both or not at all?"

Tasha laughed. "I'm not sure that's quite the threat you think it is, especially with how mad she was at you today. But yeah, we're a team. A good team."

"Hell yeah. Because, you know, I make sure I only belong to the best teams."

"I'm sure you do." She smiled, and then shot a quick glance back at the house. "Hey, you wanna get out of here? Go get a drink, maybe at McP's?"

He lifted a brow. "What about production?"

"We'll start early or go late or whatever to make up for it tomorrow. Besides, Greg confided in me that they build in extra days in the schedule just in case. We're fine."

"Well, in that case, I think a drink sounds damn good."

Especially since they'd be getting it far away from here and the cameras and at a place where he could sit Tasha in his lap in a dark corner table and devour her mouth and no one would say shit about it.

"Come on. Hop in and let's go." He moved to tug her toward the truck but she held back.

"Wait. I forgot how early it is. Will they even be open yet?" she asked.

He laughed. "Oh, yeah. Trust me. They're open."

And Raymond would be more than happy to see

that Clay dove right in and had taken his advice.

He hadn't wasted any time with Tasha. In fact, as long as they had an unexpected day off, maybe he'd take her back to her place and dive right in to something else.

It might have started out shitty, but today had turned out to be a very good day . . . and it wasn't even half over yet.

On a whim, he pulled Tasha forward and crashed his mouth over hers, kissing her like he'd wanted to for awhile now.

When he finally released her, she said, "Wow."

He smiled. "Baby, you ain't seen nothing yet."

EPILOGUE

"Good thing you're home! I was about to grill up these steaks and eat without you."

Tasha closed the front door and walked down the hall, toward the source of the booming voice that had greeted her.

Her mouth twitched with a smile as she spotted Clay in the kitchen, a dishtowel flung over his bare shoulder as, shirtless, he shucked an ear of corn.

The sight was enough to make her mouth water and it had nothing to do with the promise of the thick juicy steaks she'd spotted waiting to be grilled.

But Clay, shirtless and tempting, wasn't enough to stop her from asking, "Where are my flamingos?"

They'd started as a joke, but she'd grown fond of them over the past month.

"Relax. I moved them to the back yard. I said you could keep them, but I didn't say they could stay in front for everyone to see."

"Fine." Pouting, she put her shoulder bag on the kitchen counter and surveyed the array of fresh fruit and vegetables scattered around the kitchen.

"Where'd all this come from?"

"I went to the grocery store and then stopped by the farmer's market," he said as he dumped the cornhusks into a bag.

"Wow. I never realized you were so domestic."

Glancing at her, he cocked up a brow. "One of us needs to be."

"Hey, I told you I didn't cook the day you asked me to move in with you." For real, not for the show.

"Yeah, see, that's what I don't understand. You did all those cooking segments on your show. How could you not pick up anything after all that?"

"You watched my old shows?" A wide smile spread across her face.

He rolled his eyes. "Not the point."

She moved closer and rose on to her toes to press a kiss to his cheek. "I love you."

"I love you too." He wrapped an arm around her to pull her closer to him before he pressed a kiss to the top of her head.

"And remember, I told you I *don't* cook, not that I *can't* cook," she added with a smile.

He drew back to shoot her a scowl.

She glared right back at him. "And don't you give me that look. You love to cook and you know it. As if you'd ever let me near that new grill of yours anyway."

The damn thing smoked, barbecued, deep-fried, boiled and griddled. It did just about everything except buy the food—which Clay had obviously done in her absence.

Taking a step closer to the counter, she perused all that he'd made while she'd been gone. It looked amazing.

He'd gone to the grocery store many times before, but his visit to the farmer's market was a surprise.

In fact, the weeks she'd been living in the house with Clay after the production had finished and the cameras removed had brought one surprise after another—the biggest being that the man was a big mush when it came to animals.

She walked to the other side of the room and glanced into the crate in the corner.

"Don't you dare wake up Shelley. I just got her to sleep."

Tasha shook her head. Clay's baby, a nine-week old puppy he'd found abandoned on the beach during one of his early morning runs, snored while sleeping on her back amid a pillow and blankets.

He'd chosen her name himself, calling her Shelley because he'd found her on the beach amid the seashells.

Her tiny rounded belly was a testament to the fact Clay had made it his mission to put weight on the puppy. She'd been skin and bones when he'd found her. For two weeks he got out of bed in the middle of the night to feed her.

There was no doubt Shelley knew who'd saved her. She loved her daddy. When she was awake she followed him everywhere, like she was his shadow, and she did her best to sleep on top of him when she wasn't in her crate.

But now that she was sleeping, Clay was all Tasha's again. She moved back to him and wrapped her arms around him, laying her cheek on the hard muscles of his chest.

He wrapped both of his arms around her and kissed the top of her head again. This gentle version of Clay was also new, the opposite of the hard, violently passionate man she'd first met. Although, bits of that persona did reappear when they were in bed together.

"Where were you for so long?" he asked, squeezing her tight.

"I told you I had a hair appointment."

He frowned. "That was at one. It's like five now."

She leaned back to look up at him. "Says the man who's never had to sit through the hours-long process of getting highlights and lowlights put in his hair."

Shaking his head, he looked horrified even at the suggestion. "Yeah, no."

She laughed. "Good job sounding like a civilian though. You're doing very well."

"What are you talking about?"

"You said one and five instead of one-hundred and five-hundred hours."

His brows shot up. "Uh, thanks, but it would have been thirteen-hundred and seventeen-hundred."

"Whatever." She waved away his correction. "Anyway, I also stopped by my condo to get the mail."

Clay released his hold on her and leaned back against the counter. He crossed his arms over his chest. "You are going to change your address at one point before it's sold and the new owners move in, correct?"

"Yes, smarty pants. And for your information, I did change it on a bunch of things already. I just haven't gotten around to changing it everywhere." She reached into her bag and pulled out a padded envelope. "And if you're not nice to me, I won't let you see this."

She pulled a DVD out of the envelope and held it up.

"And what's that?" he asked, looking only mildly interested.

"It's the first episode of *Hot House*. The production company sends them out early to the media—"

He launched himself off the counter and snatched it out of her hand before striding toward the television in the corner of the living room.

"Hey! I said only if you were nice to me I'd let you see it," she teased.

He glanced back at her over his shoulder. "I'll be very nice to you later in bed. Right now, I need to see what the hell Joanne did during edits so I'm prepared for when that show airs next week."

Clay juggled the two remote controls—one for the TV and one for the DVD player. When she hung back in the kitchen and didn't follow him into the living room, he frowned back at her. "What's the matter? Don't you want to see?"

"Don't you want to eat first and watch it later?" she suggested.

His frown deepened. "No. I won't be able to enjoy those steaks until I know what I'm up against."

Tasha was the exact opposite. If they didn't watch it yet, she could still believe that she and Clay both came out of this looking great. But if they did watch it and they didn't come out looking good—what then?

Clay would be mad. Her career could be over—again.

He was still trying—and failing—to get the DVD to play. He'd figure it out eventually so she decided she might as well end his frustration and help.

She sighed and went to him.

"Give me those." She took both remotes from his hands and quickly navigated to the correct input setting. "And I want an apology from you for mocking me that I still own a DVD player when, as you put it, everyone in this decade streams instead. I told you we'd use it."

She paused, refusing to press *play* as she glanced at him and waited for her apology.

Clay blew out a huff. "I apologize. You were right. I'll make that up to you later too. Okay?"

As much as she enjoyed keeping Clay waiting, as much as she liked all the promises he was making about what pleasures were to come later when they retired to the new king-sized bed he'd bought for his room, she did as he'd asked.

She pressed the play button and tossed both remotes onto the coffee table in front of the white sofa they'd brought over from her condo.

Clay stayed standing, his eyes glued to the screen. She understood how he felt. She had too much nervous energy herself to relax, but she managed to perch on the edge of the sofa cushion as she watched.

She'd already seen the opening credits—all shots of her and Clay, looking great. That wasn't the part she was worried about. It was the actual show that concerned her, where manipulation of the raw footage could go any way the producers decided it should.

It was in the editing process where reality shows' characters were defined, both the villains and the heroes.

This first half hour episode would set up the show and determine how they'd be portrayed.

What if they'd made her look like a fool? Worse

than that, what if they had made Clay look bad?

Unable to sit still, Tasha rose and moved around the coffee table to stand next to Clay.

He uncrossed his arms and wrapped one around her. The contact made her feel better. Whatever was on this DVD, they'd deal with it together.

It felt as if she held her breath for the full twenty-two minutes of the episode waiting for—something—but there were really no surprises.

They of course made sure to make Tasha a complete fish out of water. Out of her element in a construction zone amid all the manly men.

That was fine. She could deal with that because she knew later in the project she'd learned enough to hold her own among the men. And she'd also shine during the decorating portions.

Clay came off sexy as hell. No doubt they were playing to the females who made up a good portion of the network's viewers.

As the closing credits came on, Clay let out a breath and glanced down at her. "Okay. That wasn't so bad."

"Nope," she agreed, letting out a breath of her own.

"*This season on Hot House . . .*" The voiceover caught her attention again.

Clay's too as he turned and they both watched a montage of what was going to be featured on the rest of the season's episodes.

What flashed across the screen went from bad to worse as Clay took a step closer to the television and muttered obscenities as he watched, each curse more colorful than the last.

She couldn't blame him as her cheeks burned.

All the times they'd thought they'd been fooling everyone by sneaking around, they hadn't fooled a soul.

The night vision cameras apparently had very sensitive microphones. They'd recorded her session with B.O.B. in the bathroom. Night vision had caught Clay's reaction to hearing her, as well as his stalking out of his room and into the bathroom. And then they'd recorded the sounds of the two of them having sex in the bathroom.

The preview at the end of the episode seemed to stretch on forever and the more it showed, the angrier Clay got. She could feel the rage radiating off him as her own face burned.

"Son of a bitch. They counted the condoms?" he boomed as a close-up shot of the open condom box in the medicine cabinet filled the screen.

"They were a major sponsor," Tasha offered, only to receive a glare from Clay. When the promo finally ended, she said, "At least it seems your jammer worked. I didn't see or hear anything from those nights."

"No, just the daily morning-after shot of how many condoms we'd used the night before." He shook his head. "The mother fuckers made us look like rutting animals. No, worse, we look like those idiots on those other reality shows, sneaking around to have sex and thinking no one will see."

As Clay ranted, Tasha kicked off her shoes and reached for the button on her jeans.

He finally looked at her. "What are you doing?"

"Getting naked."

"Why?" He frowned.

"Sex is extra good with you when you're angry."

"Shut up. It is not." He scowled then glanced at her from beneath lowered brows. "Is it?"

"Mmm, hmm." Her lips twitched as her bra hit the floor.

"Is that why it seemed like you were *trying* to annoy me most days we were filming?"

"Maybe." She pushed him backward until he collapsed back onto the sofa. Smiling, she crawled into his lap.

He frowned. "Dammit, woman. Stop enjoying this. I'm pissed off."

"I know. How about you just give in? You know you enjoy sex when you're angry too."

"No—"

She shook her head, cutting him off as he tried to deny it. His cock grew beneath her, proving her correct.

He ignored it and continued, "It has nothing to do with me being angry. Sex is always good."

"Yes, but not like that first night in the bathroom. When you knocked on that door, you were—"

"Insane. That wasn't anger, sweetheart. That was insanity caused by my having to be awake and alone in my bed while listening to you in the next room."

"Whatever it was, I liked it." She reached between them and trailed a finger over the fabric of the shorts covering his growing length. She slipped her hand beneath the waistband and he muttered a curse.

Eyes narrowed, he reached for her hips and pressed her tighter against him. "You know, you don't have to make me mad to drive me crazy. There's a much easier way. It might make our life together a little easier in the future."

Our life together combined with the word *future* sent

her heart fluttering. She tried not to overreact to those words and keep her cool even as her heart pounded faster.

"Oh? And what's that?" she asked with as much nonchalance as she could muster.

"All you have to do is wear those pajama pants you had at the house."

"Those? There's nothing sexy about those. They're so old I was thinking about throwing them out."

"I beg to differ. You make them very sexy."

"I guess I'd better keep them then. I'll have to sew them though, because I found a hole in the butt. Hmm. I suppose I could find some cute fabric to sew over it. Or, ooo, one of those cute embroidered patches—"

"Tasha. Stop talking." Clay rubbed his length over her most sensitive spot as his mouth crashed against hers.

In a smooth, practiced, very SEAL-like move, he flipped her over and pinned her beneath him as she shoved his shorts lower.

Those steaks, and everything else, were definitely going to have to wait a little while.

DON'T MISS THESE
SEALS IN PARADISE
TITLES

ABOUT THE AUTHOR

A top 10 *New York Times* bestselling author, Cat Johnson writes the *USA Today* bestselling Hot SEALs series, as well as contemporary romance featuring sexy alpha heroes who often wear cowboy or combat boots. Known for her creative marketing, Cat has sponsored bull-riding cowboys, used bologna to promote her romance novels, and owns a collection of camouflage and cowboy boots for book signings. She writes both full length and shorter works.

For more visit CatJohnson.net
Join the mailing list at catjohnson.net/news

89123104R00144

Made in the USA
San Bernardino, CA
20 September 2018